RAPTURE AND RUIN

KIRA COLE

1

HADLEY

THE MANAGER'S HAND DRIFTING ACROSS MY ASS AS HE escorted me into the office should have been the first sign that my day was going to go to hell.

If I'm going to pull myself out of this shit life, I need this job.

The manager says as he leans back in his chair. "We value our staff here at The Brazen," Craig crosses his arms and smirks as he finally meets my gaze. "We are under-staffed, and while you have never worked in a bar, that's okay because all you'll be doing is delivering bottles to tables. You've got the kind of face that is going to have bottles flying off the shelves."

Somehow, I don't think it's my face he's talking about.

"Thank you so much for this opportunity." I smile politely as he pulls out a hiring package. "I've wanted to work at The Brazen for a while now."

"I'm going to have you start tonight, but you need to have this filled out for your second shift. Any tips you make, you get to keep. Which means that you're going to want to smile pretty at the men and if they get a little handsy, it's not a bad thing."

I swallow the bile that rises in my throat and nod. This isn't what I ever wanted for myself, but it's the best I can do. As I reach across the desk and grab the hiring package, I can't help but think that this is a terrible idea.

If I want to finish my final year of schooling and become a kindergarten teacher, I need the kind of salary The Brazen pays its bottle service girls. I want to be the difference in children's lives.

Even if that means I spend my nights getting groped by rich men.

Craig gets up from his leather chair and rounds the desk. He opens the door, his gaze drifting down to my ass as I leave.

"Go see Kennedy at the bar. She is going to be the one training you tonight. If you have any problems, take them to her."

"Thank you," I bite my tongue as his hand grazes my hip on my way to the bar.

"You must be the new girl," A woman pops out from behind the bar, tucking her tiny tablet into the pocket of her apron. "Craig was saying that he was going to hire someone for tonight. I didn't believe him. Most women go running in the opposite direction when they meet him."

"I'm sure they do."

"I'm Kennedy. Why don't you follow me this way and we can find a uniform that will fit you? After that, we'll head up to the VIP floor and start serving the bottles."

I nod and look around the club. It's quiet right now as it is still early. The Brazen hasn't opened for the evening, but when it does, I have no doubt that it will be packed.

As one of the most exclusive clubs in Miami, there's always a line outside the door. The men and women who frequent the club often have more money than they know what to do with.

At least, that's what I read online when I was researching places to work. Personally, I try to avoid clubs as much as possible.

Kennedy leads me through a door just to the right of the bar.

We enter a staff room that matches the design of the rest of the club. It's all thick fabrics and leather seats with a dark floor and even darker walls. Everything about The Brazen screams class and luxury.

I've never been so out of place.

Kennedy pulls a stack of fabric out of a cupboard. "These look like they should fit. Go try them on and then toss the rest of your stuff in a locker. The club opens in an hour and we have a lot to do before then."

I take the uniform she shoves into my hands before disappearing behind one of the curtains.

It's only a few months until you're back in school. As long as you make enough money to pay for tuition, you can leave this place once school starts again.

That's what I keep telling myself as I take a running leap out of my comfort zone.

———

Heavy music thuds in the background as I balance a bottle on the small silver tray.

The thousand- dollar bottle of bourbon.

My hands shake slightly at the cost of the bottle, but I do my best to keep still.

The last thing I need is to lose my first paycheck to a bottle of bourbon.

"You're going to do great," Kennedy steadies my tray with one hand and adjusts the position of the bottle with the other. She centers it, watching the amber liquid slosh around the sides before settling. "Just remember to breathe."

My cheeks ache from the fake smile I've been holding for the last hour. There are still a couple of hours left of my shift, but my feet already feel like they're going to fall off.

As I make my way over to the group of men sitting on suede couches surrounding a marble table, I try not to drop the bottle. A man with dark eyes stops me in my tracks.

His gaze is enough to start chipping holes in the walls I've built so high around myself.

The way he looks at me is a promise of things yet to come. Those dark eyes seem like they can see straight to the depths of my soul. Though he doesn't smile, all I can picture are those full lips pressing against my skin. Tracing my pulse with a flick of his tongue.

Focus. I need this job.

I put the tray on the little table beside their seating area and unscrew the cap. The men watch me as I take the bottle and step inside the seating area.

My hands are sweating as I hold onto the bottle, trying to remember the hand positioning Kennedy showed me earlier.

Just a couple more steps, then you're at the table and can pour the drinks.

As I'm about to lean over the table, a hand smacks my ass. I clench my jaw and try not to react, keeping a smile on my face. When the hand hits me again, I start to turn around, ready to tell them off, but I lose my balance.

I wobble in my heels. Heat floods my cheeks as I glance at the man who caught my interest before. His dark gaze is still on me, sending my mind reeling.

The next step is the last. The heel catches in a crack between the tiles on the floor and the open bottle of bourbon slips from my grip.

Before I know what is happening, the bottle is spilling all over the man with the piercing eyes.

"What the fuck!" He jumps out of his seat, his voice booming through the VIP area.

"I'm so sorry," I put the tray on the counter that runs along the back of the room. "Let me go get something to clean that up with."

The bourbon soaks through his white dress shirt and down the front of his gray slacks. I try not to stare as his toned body is put on display. He pulls his shirt away from his chest as the men with him start to whisper.

"No need. Your fucking incompetence already speaks for itself. I can go find a fucking towel on my own."

The man glowers at me as I stand in his way. Even though I know I should step to the side and let him by, I don't.

The other men fall silent as they watch the exchange. I draw my shoulders back and stand a little taller, clasping my trembling hands in front of me.

"Please, sir, I already said I'm sorry. It was an accident. I understand that you are upset and that I have ruined your clothing, but that doesn't make it okay for you to speak to me that way."

He arches an eyebrow, his dark eyes narrowing. "Get the fuck out of my way before I get you fired."

"Calm down, man," one of the other men says, glaring

at the first man. "It's just a shirt. Hell, I will buy you a new one."

I tentatively but gratefully smile at the man who is trying to help. He nods back.

"It's the principle of the matter, Alessio. Bottle girls should not be spilling expensive alcohol on the guests. And they really shouldn't be talking back to customers the way that she has." The man I spilled the drink on shakes his head. "You're lucky if I don't have you fired after this, regardless of what my friend may think."

"Thank you." I smile at the man who is trying to help.

He gives me a small nod in return.

As I turn my attention back to the other man, my temper flares.

"I am a human being who is currently working her first shift. I apologized, and while you don't have to accept that, there is no reason to be an asshole."

That's it. I've officially lost my job. I've lit my future on fire.

I'm so fucked.

Before he can say anything else, I spin on my heel and take off for the stairs. I need to get to the staff room and take a moment to calm down before I get myself in more trouble.

"I'll take care of them," Kennedy says as she passes me with a towel in her hand. "Go take a breather and then come back out when you're ready."

"I'm going to get fired."

She smiles and takes me by the shoulders, holding me in place. "No, you're not. Just go take a breather. I promise that everything is going to be fine. It's just a spilled bottle. On my first night, I nearly lit a woman's hair on fire when she asked me to light her cigar for her."

Despite the turmoil making my stomach toss and turn,

the tight feeling in my chest eases. Kennedy lets go of me and takes a step back, tucking the towel into her pocket.

"Everything is going to be fine, Hadley. This is just one bad night."

"One bad night on a night when I needed everything to go right." My voice breaks as I look down at the ground. "I can't do this. I should have known better."

"Go get yourself cleaned up." Kennedy moves to the side, giving me enough room to pass her. "I'll handle this. It happens to the best of us."

The lump in my throat cuts off all words. I nod and take off down the stairs and into the staff room.

As soon as I'm alone, I drop down onto one of the couches and run my hands down my face.

Working at The Brazen was supposed to be the answer to losing my full-ride scholarship.

Living in a car and fighting for everything I had nearly killed me, but I got out of that life.

My parents died, life went to shit, and I figured it out.

I can figure it out again, even though I don't know how much worse tonight is going to get.

2

JOVAN

I don't know who the hell hired her, but I'm going to be the one to fire her.

"What the fuck crawled up your ass tonight?" Alessio says as he leans back against the couch cushions. "She said she was sorry and it was clearly an accident. You're just in a pissy mood tonight. Have you thought about getting laid?"

"Screw you," I say, though the corner of my mouth twitches. "You may be one of my closest friends, Alessio, but that doesn't mean that you can step into my territory and start running your mouth. This is my business and I will deal with her how I see fit."

"You're acting like an ass." Alessio crosses one leg over the other.

He might think I'm being dramatic, but I'm tired of shit like this happening at my business.

If Alessio wasn't the leader of the Italian mafia in Atlanta, I would have kicked his ass out of here tonight.

He may drive me insane, but he is one of my oldest and closest friends.

These days, it's feeling like he's one of the few people I can trust.

I'm about to respond to him when Kennedy interrupts us, walking over with the shirt I asked for. I glare at Alessio as he rolls his eyes.

"Sorry for the accident, sir," Kennedy hands me one of the black T-shirts the bartenders wear. "It's Hadley's first night and she didn't mean to spill the bottle on you. Is there anything else I can get you? Do you want me to take over service or comp the drinks?"

I sigh as I take the shirt from Kennedy. "Do you have more towels to clean this up too? You can tell your friend that she is as good as fired once I find her."

Kennedy gives me a pleading look, clasping her hands together. "Please don't fire her."

Kennedy turns to the bar and waves over one of the waitresses after piling the glass in a dustpan. Another waitress hurries over with a stack of towels in her arms. Kennedy trades the dustpan for the towels and puts them down.

"I *am* going to fire her. There is no excuse for this mess," I glower at her as I take the towels from the pile she's built on the other side of her. "I'll go deal with these. Please see to the other people here at my table and make sure that they are looked after well. Comp any food they order as well."

Kennedy nods and starts making conversation with the men and women at my table while I hurry down the stairs to the main floor of my club. The music is pounding and people are dancing in the middle of the dance floor.

I look over to the bar and grin when I see the large crowd surrounding it. We shouldn't have a problem making sales tonight, which means that by the time we close, the money I brought in this morning should be clean and ready to spend.

The more money we can clean, the tighter my grip on Miami will be. I know that I have enemies lurking around, waiting for their opportunity to snatch the city from me the same way I took it years ago.

My cartel is still too new to scare people into falling in line.

If I want to keep my position in power, I have to continuously prove that my ambition isn't my downfall. I have to make sure that the cartel is stronger than ever.

Some days, I wonder what life would be like if I had never started an uprising.

Would I be married by now? Have a family? Kids?

Truthfully, all I ever wanted in life was to make my parents proud. See the smile on their faces as I conquer goal after goal, surmount each obstacle, achieve each victory with them by my side.

If only... I shake myself out of this funk. I can't focus on this right now, I have a job to do.

As I head into the laundry room beside the kitchen, I keep an eye out for Hadley. When Craig messaged me earlier and told me that he hired a new bottle girl, I hadn't expected her to look like that.

Or run her mouth like that.

If I'm being honest, the fact that she was willing to stand up to me turned me on. These days, not many women are interested in attempting to put me in my place.

They're terrified that I will ruin their families the way I have ruined countless others.

If I had my choice, less lives would have been lost. My own family included.

I'm better off alone. Nobody can get hurt if they don't attach themselves to me.

Those few women who are brave enough to talk to me have their own motives.

Most of them just want the protection and the power that comes with being wrapped up in the cartel.

Not Hadley, though. She doesn't recognize me. She doesn't know who I am or what I have to offer her.

She is just another girl who unknowingly walked into the mouth of the lion's den.

The door to the staff room swings open, and Hadley stands there, looking like a deer caught in the headlights.

I drop the towels in the dirty laundry pile as she spins and strides to the stairs.

"Wait!" I weave through the crowd, bumping into several people. "Stop!"

She stops halfway up the stairs to the VIP area and faces me. "I'm sorry about the bottle. Please don't get me fired. I need this job."

"I wanted to apologize." I stop a couple of steps below her. "I may have come off as rude."

She crosses her arms, cocking a hip. "*May* have come across as rude? First of all, an apology starts with I'm sorry. Second, it doesn't state that things *may* have been one way or another."

I try to smother a grin at the fire burning in her eyes. Even though chasing after her — even just for this night — is a bad idea, — there's something in those hazel eyes that draws me deeper.

"I'm sorry," I take another step closer to her. " You spilled the bottle on me, but it was an accident. To make it up to me, you can dance with me."

Her cheeks flush as she tucks a strand of auburn hair behind her ear. Her full lips part slightly.

We both move to the side as people try to pass us on the stairs.

"I'm working," she says, though there is no real anger behind her voice anymore. "I have to finish out my first and last shift."

"A work ethic when you know you're going to be fired?" My voice raises slightly to be heard above the music. This girl is more surprising by the second. "Now, that's commendable. What's life without a little risk, though?"

"Grinding on a man covered in alcohol isn't my idea of a risk worth taking." Her thighs press together, her body betraying her words. "If you'll excuse me, I need to get back to my guests."

I grin and step around her, getting in her way. "Alright, so don't dance with me. Take me home with you."

"Is getting a bottle of bourbon dumped on you a kink?" She smirks when I roll my eyes. "I hate to break this to you, but I have better things to do with my night once my shift's over."

The heat of her body this close to mine sends my blood rushing south.

All I can think about are the curves of her breasts and hips. Her body beneath mine as her breathless whimpers come faster.

I take her hand, running my thumb over the back of it. "Tell you what, if the manager doesn't come over and fire you at the end of your shift, then you'll take me home with you."

She pulls her hand away and climbs another step. "Are you bribing me with what I'm sure will be sad sex just so I can keep a job?"

I follow her, invading her space again. Her eyes widen as I lean forward, dipping my head until my mouth hovers inches from hers. When her gaze connects with mine, her interest shines through.

"Trust me, you'll only be crying because you can't take another orgasm."

Her breath hitches and her gaze ignites. She squeezes her eyes shut for a moment before opening them again.

"Alright," Her voice is no more than a whisper. The corner of her mouth twitches upward as she trails a finger down my chest. "It's been a while since I've had some fun with anything other than a vibrator."

Her smirk grows as she inches my shirt up my torso. There's a little reckless part of her that is begging to break free.

I'm going to be the one who snaps the lock off the cage that holds her reckless spirit.

———

"Nice place," I say as we walk into a small apartment later that night.

It's nothing like my own penthouse, but it's a nice apartment. If you look out the window, lean to the left, and squint, you can almost see the beach. The apartment is pretty plain — like she doesn't have much to show for her life.

"You know," Hadley says as she drops her keys and purse on the kitchen counter. "You still haven't told me your name."

"I don't think it's that important." I tuck my hands into my pockets and smile. "If you really want a name, I could give you a fake one."

She kicks off her shoes. "It's really not that important. I

was just wondering which name I shouldn't call in the morning."

I chuckle and take off my own shoes, placing them beside hers. "Oh, now you have jokes?"

"Have to get through life somehow." Hadley walks into the kitchen and pulls out a bottle of tequila.

Her gaze never leaves mine as she cracks open the bottle and takes a long swig. "I normally don't do anything like this."

Grinning, I perch myself on the arm of her beige couch. "You say that like I do."

She gestures to my body. "Look at you and then tell me that you don't."

"I can't."

Hadley leans against the counter and fidgets with the hem of her shorts. "Exactly. I still can't believe you were right about me not getting fired. That bottle was expensive."

The last thing I want to talk about right now is that damn bottle.

I get up and close the distance between us. Her breath hitches as I take the tequila from her and set it on the counter. "If you want me to leave, you can tell me. I'm not going to make you do anything that you don't want to do."

Suspicion lingers in her eyes as I tower over her.

"I'm serious, Hadley. I won't call into your work and insist that you're fired either."

Her eyes narrow. "How do you know my name?"

"The other bottle girl told me when she was cleaning up the spill." I put my hands on her hips, my thumbs brushing the sliver of visible skin above the waistband of her shorts.

She trembles, her head tilting back. "You're really serious about this?"

I lean over to graze her earlobe with my teeth. "Very."

Her hands work their way up my chest to link behind my neck.

I pull back to look at her, and it feels like my entire world has shattered.

I'm going to have to fire her after this. I can't have her working with me and looking at me like this. Like I'm... worthy of being with someone. Like she's about to embrace the darkest parts of me.

I push away all thoughts of what's going to happen once we're done fucking. Instead, I close the distance between us and focus on the way her mouth feels against mine.

Hadley's fingers weave through my hair and she pulls me closer. Her soft moans as my tongue slides against hers have my cock hardening. She gasps as my cock digs into her. I take the opportunity to tangle my tongue with hers, the taste of her burning itself into my memory.

I press against her, pinning her between the counter and my body as my hands slide beneath her shirt.

Her skin is soft against my fingertips as I work my way up to the underside of her breasts. She moans louder as I slip my hands beneath her lacey bra and roll her nipples between my fingers.

Her nipples peak beneath my touch, her attraction to me undeniable. I want to peel off her clothing and tease her nipples until she's on the edge of an orgasm.

"So responsive," I say as I kiss my way down her neck.

She arches her back, pushing her breasts harder into my hands as I massage the soft flesh. Hadley's fingers claw at my shoulders as I suck on the sensitive skin at the base of her neck.

"You're wearing too much clothing," her voice is breathless as her hands slide down my body. She digs her nails into my skin, making me shudder.

I pull off her shirt as she flicks open the button on my slacks.

Our clothing pools in a pile at our feet as we strip each other.

Her nails rake over my skin, sending a shiver down my spine as I lift her onto the counter.

Her legs part as I kneel on the ground, my fingers grazing over her wet core. Hadley spreads her legs a little wider as my fingers circle her clit. Her wetness coats my fingers as I tease her.

She runs her fingers through my hair, pulling it as she grinds her pussy against my touch.

"More, please." Hadley hooks one leg over my shoulder, arching her back. Her heel digs into my shoulder, pulling me closer to her.

"You want to come on my tongue?" I give her a teasing lick to accentuate my words before returning my fingers to her clit.

"Yes."

"Say it, Hadley. Tell me what you want."

She whimpers as I press my thumb against her clit. "Please. I want to come on your tongue."

"Good girl."

As I replace my fingers with my tongue, her legs squeeze my shoulders. I press my fingers into her, pushing against her inner walls as I thrust. My tongue flicks against her clit as my fingers move faster.

When her pussy starts pulsating around me, I flatten my tongue against her clit. Hadley's moans fill the room as she comes, coating my fingers with her wetness.

"You look so pretty when you come," I stand between her legs, my fingers still slowly thrusting into her. "I want to feel that tight little pussy milking my cock as I come."

"Bedroom. Down the hall on the right," she says as her legs wrap around my waist.

I pick her up and carry her down the hall, kissing her neck and chest while her legs tighten around me. Her nails dig into my back and I'm sure there will be marks there in the morning.

Lust fills Hadley's gaze as I toss her onto the bed. Her legs part and her hands start roaming her body. She teases her nipples as I crawl onto the bed and hover over her.

As I line my cock up with her entrance, she hooks one leg around my hip. I groan as I press into her, feeling her pussy clench around me.

Hadley rocks her hips, trying to take me deeper as I hold back.

"Fuck," My voice is raspy as I give her long and slow strokes.

Hadley lifts her hips, meeting me thrust for thrust.

I pull her harder against me as I thrust faster and harder.

Her inner walls clamp down around me as another orgasm washes over her.

All it takes is the feeling of her pussy squeezing my cock to make me come.

I groan as I pump into her, driving deeper until I'm completely spent.

As I lay in bed beside her, my fingers tracing up and down her thigh, I feel horrible for what I'm about to say.

Though, I am attracted to her, which is exactly why I can't have her near me.

"Hadley," I get out of bed and gather my clothing. "This was fun and all, but it's not going to work out. There are a few perks of owning The Brazen and one of those is control over the staff."

Her eyes widen and her lips part. Water brims in her eyes as she clutches the blanket to her chest. "What are you doing? What are you saying?"

"This was your first and last night working at The Brazen. Your paycheck will be mailed to you."

3

HADLEY

I GLARE AT THE GRAY STONE WALLS OF THE BRAZEN bright and early Monday morning.

Though I don't know what my plan is going to be once I get in there, I know that I'm not going to take this lying down.

Even if Jovan Aguilar is the leader of the Aguilar cartel.

Sighing, I weigh my options for the millionth time since I found out who the man I slept with was.

On one hand, I can confront him. On the other hand, I could find a new job.

Then there is the concern of who he is and what connections he has.

If I risk irritating him, he could make my life hell.

As soon as he walked out Friday night, I searched the internet for any mention of the owner of The Brazen. It had taken a little more digging to find a picture of him but once I did, I knew that he was telling the truth.

He is the owner of The Brazen and I am lucky that I'm not dead.

The man I slept with was both my boss and one of the

deadliest people to reside in Miami in the last several decades.

I bite my bottom lip as I consider going back home. Nobody would ever know that I was here. I didn't have to get myself wrapped up in the cartel after so many years of avoiding it.

Hell, the last time I was around anyone associated with the cartel was on the night my parents overdosed seven years ago.

And now I'm debating marching into the lion's den and demand — or beg — for my job back.

After taking a deep breath, I enter through the employee door. The kitchen staff barely look at me as I weave around the equipment in the room before heading out into the main club.

There are a few people meeting at one of the tables on the far side of the club, piles of money in front of them. One of them looks up as I pass them and head for the door that leads to The Brazen's offices.

I don't stop walking down the long hall until I reach the one with Jovan's name on it. There is a long pause between when I knock on the door and when it opens, but as soon as it does, the few sentences I had prepared die on my lips.

Jovan sighs and crosses his arms, leaning against the doorframe as he looks down at me. His gaze is enough to stop me in my tracks. All I can think about is the way he looked at me when he was buried inside me.

Get ahold of yourself. You came here for a reason.

"Can I help you?" he asks, his tone gruff. "I was sure that I had fired you, yet here you are. Would you like to explain why?"

"I want my job back. Spilling the bourbon was an accident and you can take the cost out of my first pay."

Jovan scoffs. "I want nothing from you. I told you that you were fired. Find another job, sweetheart. One where you aren't going to be spilling bottles on some very powerful men. You're too goody-good for a place like this. You should be working at some bubblegum pink-colored clothing store, talking about the men you see in movies. Maybe saving bunnies. Sure as shit not working in a club."

"I've been brushing shoulders with bad shit my entire life. I know who you are and that isn't going to scare me away from working here."

If he knew what's happened in my life, he wouldn't think I'm too innocent to play his little game.

It's clear that he wants to be in a power position over me, and he's in one. He is the one who gets to say whether or not I have a job. Allowing me to have my job back directly impacts my ability to return to university and finish studying.

Being a kindergarten teacher is something I always wanted. I've done what it takes to get there, I just have to do whatever else it will take to see it through.

If that means that I have to play nice with Jovan and hope that he gives me my job back, then that is what I'll do.

Creating a difference in a child's life is worth giving up my pride.

He raises an eyebrow. "And what do you think your colleagues will think when they find out you've been sleeping with the boss?"

I shrug and mimic his posture. "I don't think it will matter much since that was a mistake that happened one time. Besides, I'm sure I'm not the only one. Is that how you get ahead here?"

His eyes narrow, and for a moment, I think he's going to kick me out. Not that I would blame him. I'm being a pain, and he did fire me only to have me show up at his business unannounced.

"Why do you want this job? There are dozens of other clubs within a ten minute drive. Why is The Brazen so important?"

"It's an exclusive club. The tips are better. The bottle service girl base pay is better. I need several thousands of dollars to be able to afford my last year of school."

I'm proud of myself when my voice doesn't waver.

Jovan looks significantly less impressed, but he still hasn't told me to leave yet. That is enough to give me hope.

"What you need money for isn't my problem." He walks inside the office and glances over his shoulder.

I follow him and shut the door behind me. "Please, Jovan. I really need this job. I won't say anything about sleeping with you and I'll work hard."

He sighs and sits behind his desk, glancing at a paper on top of it. When he looks at me, I can see the words he is about to say. He's about to tell me to leave.

He doesn't care that I need money and I can't blame him for that. Everyone needs money. My needing money isn't any more important than anyone else's.

Not to him.

"Look, Hadley, this isn't the kind of place you should be. There are dangerous people in and out of here all the time."

"There are dangerous people all over Miami. Wherever I go, I'm going to run into any number of things. I want to be here, though."

Jovan runs his hand along his jaw before giving a sharp nod. "Alright. I'll give you your job back. But there are conditions. I don't want you to become a problem. I have enough of them on my hands."

"I won't be a problem." I stand in front of his desk and tuck my hands into the pockets of my shorts. "I promise."

"I know. There will be consequences if you do. You will not speak to me while you work here unless absolutely necessary and nobody is to know about the night I spent with you. If you break either of these terms, I will fire you on the spot."

Swallowing hard, I nod.

I have no desire to waste time talking to him after what happened the other night. And as for not talking about it, I have no problem saying yes. There is no way that I would tell anybody all the details of what happened.

I'm too humiliated. Jovan played me for a fool and it doesn't bother him at all.

"Easy enough. Is there anything else?" I ask, picking at a loose thread in my pocket.

"Yes. Part of your new job is being my personal bottle service girl. Any and all meetings I take in this club will require you to be there. I want you under my thumb where I can watch you and make sure that you're not screwing up. Again."

The corner of his mouth turns upward as my pride takes a hit. He's getting some sort of sick enjoyment out of this.

Not that it surprises me.

"You know, if you prefer, instead of bottle girl, maybe I would be willing to keep you around for other purposes," Jovan said, a slow smile spreading across his face.

"With all due respect, no, thank you," I say, my voice tight as I try to remain professional. My mouth has already put me in enough trouble as it is. I would gain nothing by saying what's running through my mind. That he can take his deal and go straight to hell. That waiting on him hand and foot sounds like a nightmare. That I wouldn't even mind his proposal if he hadn't been such an asshole after we were done.

That I haven't been able to stop thinking about us sleeping together. Although, sharing what me and my vibrator do in my alone time seems like a bad idea.

Jovan smirks and leans back in his chair, kicking his feet up on the edge of his desk. The look he gives me makes me think that he knows exactly what I'm thinking about.

"You can tell me to go fuck myself," Jovan says, chuckling to himself. "I wouldn't blame you for that."

"What's the point on wasting anymore energy on you?"

Instead of waiting for an answer, I leave his office and head through the club to the door. I have my job back. I don't need to spend more time around Jovan today.

Working with him is going to be hard enough.

I need to keep reminding myself who I'm dealing with and what he's capable of. Though I can't find any record of his serving prison time, it doesn't mean that he's not a dangerous man.

He's the leader of the cartel and he could kill me if he wanted.

The stupid side of me is the one that's willing to admit knowing who Jovan is turns me on far more than it should.

There is something about the darkness in him that seduces the darkness lingering in me.

4

JOVAN

I POUR MYSELF A GLASS OF WHISKEY AS A PETITE blonde trails her hand down my arm. Once upon a time, her touch would have made me feel something. But just like the woman who had been in my office last week, I can't be less interested.

The only person I keep picturing naked is the redhead who stormed her way into my office and made it clear she wouldn't leave until I gave her the job back.

Fucking Hadley. She is going to be a thorn in my damn side.

"What's on your mind?" Giana asks, running her hands up and down my chest. She starts to fiddle with the buttons on my shirt, pouting as she looks up at me.

"Not tonight, Giana. Not any night ever again either. That was a one-time thing. It's not going to happen again."

I down my drink and step away from her. She reaches for me again even as I swat her hands away. As I set the glass on the counter, I think about how easy it would be to make her disappear. She doesn't have anyone who would miss her and she would no longer be my problem.

I need her to get me information. I can't be done with her yet.

"Why are you acting like this, baby?" she asks, her voice a purr. I'm sure it's supposed to be sexy but it just makes my stomach twist.

"We have an arrangement that is based on information. You give me information and I don't give your pimp information on where you are every Tuesday night. Now, start talking."

"I don't know what you want me to say," she says, the seductive tone gone. "And if you tell him where I am, I'll gut you."

Chuckling, I close the distance between us and wrap my hand around her neck. Her eyes grow wide as I bend her back over the counter, squeezing her throat until she starts clawing at my hand.

"Let's get one thing clear, Giana." I press on her throat a little harder. "If you ever think that you can threaten me again, think twice. I'm going to allow you to live this time because you are still useful to me, but if it happens again, I will kill you."

Giana nods, still clawing at my hand. I give her neck another squeeze for good measure before letting go and stepping back.

"Now," I say as I cross my arms and look at her. "Do you have information for me or have you just come here to waste my time?"

Giana runs her hand over her neck. "Felix Domingos has been spotted back in Miami. I didn't think it was true until I was working at a club the other night. I was up there dancing and he sat right in front of me."

"Did he say anything to you? Does he know that you work for me?"

"No," she says, shaking her head. "He looked like he was there for a good time but he didn't seem interested in much else."

"Which club?"

Felix is smart. He wouldn't be showing his face at any of the well-known and popular clubs in the area. Not after I killed his family and took control of Miami for myself.

Now it looks like he's back to try to reclaim the city for the Domingos cartel.

"Cargo. That old one downtown. Where the newer dealers are spending time at right now."

Cargo is the kind of club people go to if they want information and discretion. It's one of the clubs that I started sending Giana to shortly after I took control of Miami.

I study Giana for a moment, looking for any sign of a lie on her face. When I don't see the telltale squint of her eyes, I head to my bedroom. She waits in the kitchen as I open the safe and grab her payment.

The second I hand her the money, she takes off for the door.

"Good work, Giana." I frown as she looks over her shoulder at me. "See what else you can find out about Felix."

"Yes, sir."

"And Giana?" I stare right at her when I say, "If anyone finds out I'm aware he is back in town, I know on whose door I'll come knocking. Understood?"

She nods before spinning around and yanking the door open. It slams closed behind her, leaving me alone in my penthouse apartment with nothing but the silence to comfort me.

I sigh and look at my empty glass on the counter. I could refill it and drink while I figure out what to do about the Domingos heir, but that's not going to help anything.

Instead, I grab the glass and throw it against the far wall. I thought that I had dealt with the Domingos family once and for all. Though I know Felix is still alive, I didn't think that he would make the mistake of coming back to Miami.

Not when he knows that there is a price for his head.

I stare at the shattered glass on the ground, a million different thoughts racing through my mind.

Right now, I don't want to go after Felix. Not yet. I need to know what he is planning so I can make sure it never comes to fruition.

If he is building support, I need to find out who the traitors are. I can't afford to lose Miami. My cartel is still new to the area — though it has been eleven years since I took control from the Domingos cartel.

If Felix topples the Aguilar cartel, I won't be able to rebuild elsewhere.

Miami is my life and I'm not going to let him take it from me without a fight.

He can live for now, but when the time is right...

RUNNING IS ONE OF THE FEW THINGS THAT CLEARS MY mind. After cleaning the glass off the floor, I took off for the longest run I've had in a long time. My heart is pounding as I run through the streets of Miami, sweat dripping down my face.

When I stop in front of Hadley's apartment building at the end of my run, I have no clue what I'm doing or why I'm here. I had put my headphones on and started running with no destination in mind.

I stare up at the building, looking at the windows until I see her. She's dancing around to something, a smile on her face and a glass of wine in her hand. As I watch her for a few minutes, I consider leaving her alone.

Even though she seems like she can handle herself, all the trouble that comes with my life is more than any normal person would be able to handle.

While I should walk away and head back to my own home, I don't. Instead, I head to the door and press a random button on the intercom. The person doesn't bother to answer before they press the button to buzz me into the building.

I head up the stairs to Hadley's floor, still trying to figure out what I'm doing and why.

I know I should go home, but I keep walking until I'm standing outside her apartment door. I can hear soft music playing inside as the hallway light flickers above me.

It's well after midnight and she is awake, dancing around by herself. I want to ask her what she is doing and why she can't sleep. There is something about her that fascinates me. I want to learn more.

There's a charity gala the club is hosting in a week. I can invite her to go to that with me. She needs money. If I offer her a bonus, she might just agree.

I convince myself that's why I knock on her door, though deep down I know better.

Right now, I'm not ready to even begin trying to untangle the strange mess of emotions I feel when it comes to her. Not when I've only been around her for a short amount of time yet still can't get her out of my head.

Through the door, I can hear her moving. The floorboards squeak beneath her feet and the door rattles slightly against the frame. I hear the slide of the chain before the door opens.

"You know it's the middle of the night, right?" Hadley asks, completely disregarding a greeting in favor of a glare. "Normally, people visit other people in the middle of the day. And that first person typically knows that the other one is coming over."

I smirk and shrug, tucking my hands in my pockets. "I was in the neighborhood."

She scoffs and steps aside to open the door a little wider. "Come in. I don't want to wake up my neighbor. We just got her baby to sleep a few minutes ago."

"You were helping your neighbor put her baby to sleep?"

I follow her into the little apartment, trying not to think about the asshole move I pulled the last time I was here. I should have been nicer to her — at least in that regard — but I had wanted to make sure she knew I wasn't the kind of person she should be around.

And now I'm the one thinking of ways to keep her around, thinking about her like she needs some damn white knight to come in and save her.

The fire in her eyes when she challenges me makes it clear that she doesn't need anyone to save her.

"Yeah, she's a single mother. Works two jobs to keep food and formula on the table. I help her when I can." Hadley locks the door behind me before heading to the living room.

"Why not nanny for someone instead of serving alcohol to assholes?"

She turns the music off. "Jovan, you've made it clear that my personal life is of no interest to you."

"And now I'm asking you."

Hadley looks skeptical as she perches herself on the arm of her couch, crossing one long leg over the other. My gaze traces the curves of her body, remembering the way her soft skin felt beneath my touch.

"I love kids but being a nanny isn't going to make me enough money in time. The Brazen is known for a good base rate and clientele who tips well."

"And you think that finishing school is going to get you where you want to go?"

"What's with the sudden interest in my life? And why are you showing up in the middle of the night to ask me about it?"

I can see her putting her walls back up. The small glimpse of herself that she's allowed is the only one I'm going to get.

It only makes me more curious about her. What happened in her life that made her this closed off to others?

"No interest." I unlock the door and open it up. "I have a gala in a week at The Brazen. We're going to be raising money for charity. I'll send you an outfit to wear."

Confusion crosses her face. "Is that what you do for all your staff?"

"Nope. I need a date to the event."

Hadley scoffs. 'I'm not going to be your date. I don't want anything to do with you in that capacity at all. It's highly outside the realm of professionalism."

I grin and walk over to her. "If you think that's unpro-fessional, wait until I get through with you."

She glares at me as she puts her hand on my chest and pushes me back a step. "If you think that is going to intimi-date me, try again. I've dealt with worse than you."

I chuckle and shake my head, reaching out to wrap a

strand of her red hair around my finger. I pull on it lightly before dropping the strand and walking to the door.

When I look back at her, she looks like she's ready to kick my ass. "Go with me to the gala, Hadley."

"No."

"I'll give you an extra thousand dollars to be my date. You said that you need the money. I can give you the money."

I can see the fight behind her eyes as she wavers a moment before she nods. I see the shame on her face but clearly she needs the money more than her pride.

"Excellent. I'll meet you at The Brazen on Friday."

Hadley sighs. "Please just leave."

I look at her for a moment longer before walking out the door and shutting it behind me. One man passes me, keeping his eyes trained on the floor while I wait for Hadley to lock her door.

Once I hear the lock twist in the door, I head for the stairs.

For the first time since Giana's visit earlier today, I finally feel like I can go home and go to sleep.

Though I don't know why, being around Hadley soothes my restless mind.

5

HADLEY

As the limo stops in front of The Brazen Friday night, I start to panic. Nothing about this situation is right. I shouldn't be going to a charity gala with my boss at the business he owns.

I shouldn't be potentially entangling myself with the leader of a cartel. Not after all the shit from my past. After what happened with my parents.

Who knows where my life would have gone if they hadn't spent their lives chasing a high that always left them unsatisfied.

The door opens and the limo driver stands on a red carpet, extending his hand to me. Even though I want to hide deeper in the car, I know that Jovan is the kind of man who will come drag me out of it if he has to.

It's as if he can sense my hesitation from the club. The doors open and the press that has been invited starts snapping pictures and shouting questions. Jovan walks out with an easy smile and a suit tailored to fit his muscled body.

When a man looks like him, it's hard to believe that he would be the head of a cartel.

I step out of the limo, teetering slightly on my heels before regaining my composure. Jovan walks over to me and I take a deep breath.

I'm not ready for this. Not even a little bit. I should turn around now and run back to the limo.

"Don't even think about it," Jovan says as he stops in front of me and holds out his hand. "Come on. The red carpet isn't as scary as you think it is."

I glance at the canopy lined with lights and crystals that hangs above the carpet. It's shining like stars against the night sky.

"It looks pretty scary. This isn't the kind of thing that normal people do. This shit is reserved for movie stars and billionaires."

He chuckles as his gaze drifts down my body, lingering on the cut-outs on the sides of the black gown. When he looks up at me, heat pools in my core. That look is the kind that promises a night I won't forget.

It's the same look he gave me when I brought him home that night.

"Well," Jovan says as I put my hand in his and allow him to lead me down the red carpet. "I'm not a movie star."

I lean closer to him, feeling the tension flowing between us. "Yeah, but how many of those billions of dollars are clean?"

Jovan chuckles, letting go of my hand to wrap his arm around my waist. The men stationed on either side of the doors pull them open to reveal the club.

It looks nothing like it does at night. There are thick black and white linens draping the walls. Thick gold fabric breaks up the monotony of the rest of the room. People gather around in gowns and suits, drinks in their hands as soft music plays from a string quartet at the front of the room.

"There is no way that this is The Brazen," I say as I look up at him.

Jovan smiles and greets several people as we head to the bar. We approach a man. I don't know him, but I've seen him before. It's the man who tried to stand up for me the night I spilled alcohol on Jovan.

"Alessio Marchetti, meet Hadley James." Jovan gestures between us with a smile on his face.

"Hadley, nice to properly meet you. I take it you still have your job?" Alessio says, a slight tilt to his lips. Not quite a smile, but the ghost of one as he lifts his flute of champagne to his lips. His eyes sparkle with mischief as he takes a sip. "I have a few other associates I need to meet with, but I hope to see you again later this evening."

Alessio nods to Jovan before disappearing into the crowd. Jovan keeps his arm around my waist as we continue our trek to the bar.

"Why was it so important that I meet him?" I ask, glancing over my shoulder to look at Alessio. I scan the crowd but he is nowhere to be found.

"He's the kind of man you can count on in an emergency. I'm not going to lie. You being seen with me is dangerous in a sense. Alessio might live in Atlanta, but he can be here in a hurry if you're ever in trouble. I'll give you his number later."

"Great," I say as we push through the people to the bar. "Just what I need. Risking my life for you."

Kennedy eyes me with a knowing smile on her face as she hands us flutes of champagne. Her gaze darts between us before settling on me.

"Having a good night?" she asks, her grin growing when my cheeks start to heat up.

"We never mention this again," I say as I narrow my eyes. "Never. As far as you know, this never happened."

Kennedy laughs and rolls her eyes. "You're going to have to give me all the dirty details later."

Jovan is smirking as he steers me away from the bar and toward the second floor. We climb the stairs together, slipping through a group of people at the top. Lining the second floor are tables filled with things that are being auctioned off. There is a little form beside each prize where people write down their bids.

As I look at a stunning set of earrings, Jovan leans over beside me. He picks up the pen and scribbles something down on the form.

"What are you doing?" I ask when I look down and see the bid for fifty thousand dollars.

"You're practically drooling over them. You know, if I win, you're going to have to find a nose ring that matches."

His playful behavior catches me off guard. He seems more relaxed than he has been since I met him. I don't know what to make of the new energy.

Much like I don't know what to make of this entire night.

When he asked me to be his date, I thought that he was going insane. When the black dress arrived at my apartment, along with shoes and three sets of gold earrings to fill each of my piercings, I just about lost my mind.

This isn't the kind of life I live.

Even though I don't want him to think that I am the kind of person who will do whatever it takes to get ahead, he offered me a thousand dollars.

A thousand dollars to put on a dress and go on a date with him is a small ask.

At least, that's what I keep telling myself.

Although, most people think that making a deal with the devil is fine until it isn't.

"I have to go meet some people," Jovan says as he steps away. "Do your best to charm people and convince them to give the disadvantaged youth of Miami more money."

He disappears before I have a chance to protest, leaving me in a room full of people I don't know.

I take a deep breath before I head downstairs where the main party is. I weave through the crowd, stopping every now and then to talk to one person or another. It's easy to talk about the auction upstairs when they ask what Jovan is bidding on.

Being in a room with these people makes me sick. The only thing that matters to them is the money. Who is spending what, who has the most, and who owns what. Everything is a status symbol to them.

It's everything I've never wanted.

As I start to do another lap around the room, I see a man I never thought I would see again. My stomach erupts in a flurry of butterflies as I stare at him, watching him talk to the people around him.

He looks up from his conversation, his gaze darting around the room before landing on me. I turn and try to disappear into the crowd, though I know it's too late.

Carlos Ruiz has seen me and he's going to track me down.

If I keep moving, I might be able to avoid him until it's time to leave. I don't know how long I have to be at the gala for, but I doubt Jovan will make me stay until it ends.

"There you are," Carlos says, stepping in front of me

and stopping me in my tracks. "I haven't seen you since your parents' house burned down. Funny how that works, isn't it? They overdose. You find them and call me. And then the house goes up in flames before I can get there."

"Who knows what happened," I say, giving him a polite smile. I take a sip of champagne to try and calm my nerves. My heart is racing as he chuckles and shakes his head.

"You know, I wouldn't have thought that you had it in you."

"You don't know what you're talking about." My voice breaks, and I take another sip of my drink.

Don't let him see your fear.

"If you're done bothering my date, Carlos, I have a conversation that I need to have with her. I would suggest that you leave the gala. I don't remember inviting you, and as you know, my events are invitation only."

Carlos sneers at Jovan, nodding once before heading for the door. I wait until he is gone before drinking the last of my champagne. Jovan gives me a curious look as I shove the glass into his hand before walking away.

I need a minute to myself before I can deal with Jovan again.

"Hadley, wait."

Ignoring him, I keep walking until I enter the staff room. Something breaks outside the door seconds before Jovan walks in. He stares at me for a moment before turning and locking the door.

"Do you want to tell me what was going on out there?" he asks, taking off his suit jacket and tossing it on one of the couches. "Because that looked like you knew Carlos. He's not a good man to know."

"Neither are you," I say.

The room feels like it's closing in around me. I take several deep breaths, trying to slow my racing heart.

"Hadley, what's going on? You look like you're about to throw up. Do you need to go home?"

"I'm fine." I look up at him, trying not to lose it. The last person I want to talk about Carlos with is his boss. "I just need a distraction."

He looks skeptical as he reaches out to grab my hand. "Why don't you sit down? I can get you a glass of water and then we can talk about whatever it is that's worrying you like this."

"I don't need a glass of water," I say, my words coming out sharper than I meant them. I run a hand through my loose waves and sigh. "I'm sorry. I shouldn't be snapping at you when you're just trying to help. I don't want to talk about what that was out there."

"What do you want?" he asks as he sits down on the couch, leaning back against the cushions.

My core clenches at the way he's looking at me. His gaze travels slowly up and down my body, making it clear that he is taking his time enjoying the view.

Even as wrong for each other as we are, he excites me. He makes me feel wanted.

That's why I close the distance between us and straddle his lap, the loose skirt falling around his lap. Jovan's eyebrows raise as I loop my arms over his shoulders. His hands slide beneath the skirt, gripping my hips as his cock hardens beneath me.

He groans as I roll my hips. Jovan's fingers press into the flesh of my hips, dragging me against him.

There is fire in his eyes as his hands start exploring my body beneath the dress. His fingers work their way up and down my thighs. Everywhere he touches feels like it's on fire.

"Is this really what you want right now?" he asks, his voice husky as I get out of his lap and reach behind my back. I pull down the zipper and let the dress fall, the fabric pooling on the ground.

"I don't know," I say as I straddle his lap again. "You tell me."

His fingers dip between my legs, sliding the silky material of my underwear out of the way. I moan as he circles my clit slowly, applying more pressure with each swirl of his fingers.

"You're soaking wet for me," he says, his voice gruff as his fingers leave my body to pull his cock out of his pants. "But we're going to have to be quick. Someone is going to come looking for us soon. We don't want them to find you getting yourself off on my cock."

He strokes his cock as he speaks, his dark eyes burning a hole through me. Jovan's other hand grips the back of my head.

When our mouths meet, I moan. His tongue slips inside my mouth, moving against mine as he lines his cock up with my pussy. He teases me with the head, sliding it along my slick core before pushing into me.

"You're going to need to be quiet when you come." Jovan pulls my hair, making my back arch as he thrusts into me.

I roll my hips, meeting his thrusts as tension starts to build. My pussy is pulsing around him as he drives deeper into me. He pulls my hair harder as he slams into me. I grip his shoulders, my fingers digging into the soft material of his shirt.

"Come for me," he says, his other hand slipping

between my legs to press against my clit.

He dips his head to my chest, pulling a nipple into my mouth. I moan and move my hips faster, my orgasm building. When he switches to the other nipple, biting down gently, my orgasms races through me.

Jovan groans, his hands leaving my hair and clit to grab both hips as he pumps into me harder and faster. His cock is throbbing as he stills inside me. My pussy is still clenching around him as he comes.

"We're going to have to get cleaned up before we go back out there," Jovan says as I get off his lap and collect my dress.

"Pretty sure you're not supposed to use the staff showers for sex."

He gives me a wicked grin. "Weren't supposed to use the staff couch either. Here's the offer, Hadley. One final fuck and then we are done sleeping with each other. Got it?"

I look at him, weighing my options. I've already slept with him twice. A third time isn't going to hurt.

But I know that's not true. It could hurt a whole lot. I could lose my job. The people I work with might start to hate me. We could get caught.

The thought of getting caught only intensifies the lust flowing through my body as I take him by the hand and lead him to the showers.

This is the last time I'm going to let him past my defenses.

After tonight, he is my boss and nothing more.

Tell that to the fantasies circling through your mind when you're in bed at night.

As we step into the shower together, I try not to think about the massive mistake I know I'm making.

6

JOVAN

For the last three weeks, I've barely seen Hadley. Hell, the only way I know she received the earrings from the auction is the way the box was left on my desk the following day.

No note. Nothing to tell me that she didn't want them. It was as cold and impersonal as it could get.

It was exactly what our relationship needed to be.

My interest in her is still growing, but only through the rare glimpses I get of her. She is my bottle girl when I meet with clients. Other than that, I don't see her often. Hadley is good at getting lost in a crowd.

It only makes me wonder where and why she honed that particular skill to perfection.

Even now, as she leaves for the day, she makes sure to avoid anywhere I might be. I watch her on the cameras as she says goodbye to the bouncers before heading for her car.

The sun is just starting to rise as she sits behind the wheel, staring at the club. For a brief second, her gaze darts to the camera.

Does she know I'm watching?

I always watch the camera to make sure that my employees leave without hassle after the club closes for the night. The bouncers walk the staff to their cars, but I like to keep watch from afar.

Though some people might describe me as a bad man — and they wouldn't be wrong — I care for my staff. For the most part, they are good people. They all have families waiting for them to come home.

I won't allow them to be taken away from their families like mine was taken away from me.

After a few more minutes of sitting in her car, Hadley gets out and starts walking. She glances over her shoulder before turning a corner and disappearing out of the camera's sight and into the early morning.

"For fuck's sake," I say, locking my computer before getting up and heading for the doors to follow her.

Neither of the bouncers say anything to me as I walk outside and follow her. She doesn't seem to notice me as she turns another corner.

I keep my distance from her, wondering where she is going.

Is she working for Felix? It seems like too much of a coincidence for her to start working for me once he comes back to town.

It's not the first time that I've thought Hadley might not be who she says she is. I doubt it will be the last time that I suspect her of it either.

There's a lot of things that don't make sense about that woman. Too many pieces of the puzzle are still missing.

I don't like missing pieces. Missing pieces are how my cartel is put in jeopardy.

Hadley walks quickly, looking behind her every now and then. I keep my head down and stay several feet behind her, making sure she doesn't see me the few times she does look over her shoulder.

She keeps walking, farther and farther away from downtown.

The houses around us look like they've been neglected for years. Grass grows high and fences are falling apart. Several of the houses have broken windows. Even more are covered with graffiti.

There are kids playing, though most of them look like the kind of kids that grow up to join cartels.

What the hell is Hadley doing here?

She keeps walking until she stops in front of a house that looks like it's been ravaged by a fire. The entire exterior is covered in scorch marks and there isn't a single window intact.

I hide behind a car resting on cinder blocks and watch as she looks around. It's too early in the morning for anyone other than the kids to be outside.

I doubt they're supposed to be outside either, but I know sometimes outside is happier than at home.

Hadley grabs onto one of the window ledges and hauls herself up. She slides inside the house like it's something she's done a million times before.

The hell. Whose house is she breaking into?

I didn't think that Hadley had something like that in her but now I'm starting to see that I may have been wrong about her. That recklessness I saw in her the first night we met is showing again.

It's what prompts me to dash out from behind the car and follow her into the house.

Though I don't see her when I enter, I take a moment to look around. Furniture is burned and soot coats the walls and ceiling. There are a couple holes in the hardwood floors where a fire once burned through.

Weeds and animals have started taking over the space. A mouse scurries by with something in its mouth, disappearing into a hole in the wall.

"What are you doing here?" Hadley asks, appearing in the living room with me. She looks around, her eyes slightly watery.

"I could ask you the same thing. This doesn't seem like the kind of place you would spend your time."

Her cheeks turn pink as she glares at me. "Because you know everything about me, right? Sleeping together a few times means that you get to judge what is and isn't like me without giving much consideration to the fact that you don't really know me."

I shrug and look around. "Alright, then. What is this place?"

"That's still not any of your business." Hadley crosses her arms, her eyes narrowing. "Why did you follow me here?"

"I watch the cameras when the staff leaves. Saw you sit in your car and then get out and start walking. Figured I should follow you and see what you were up to."

"Ah, yes," she says, her tone dripping with sarcasm. "Because the leader of a fucking cartel really gives a shit about the people below him. Don't pretend that you followed me because you give a shit about me."

"No, I came out here because I can't trust you and I don't know if you are going to fuck me over or not."

I brush past her and walk into the hallway. I dodge a hole in the floor before heading into the kitchen. There are still dishes sitting out — though most of them are broken or cracked. It looks like the fire didn't quite get this far into the house before it was put out.

As I look around the room, Hadley sighs.

"Is there a problem with my being here?" I ask as I open a door in the back of the kitchen that leads into a tiny laundry room.

"The problem is that you're invading my life and making yourself at home in it. I don't want you to be nosing around my business. You agreed that we were going to be professional."

I look down at the floor and see a trap door. Carved into the door is the symbol of the Domingos cartel. As I turn to face Hadley, I keep my expression blank.

"No," I say as I walk out of the room and close the door behind me. "I said that I wasn't going to make you come again. I never said anything about invading your personal life."

"I wish you would stop it. There's nothing for you to see."

I step closer to her, only a few inches separating us. Her chest brushes against mine as she tilts her head back slightly to look up at me. My fingers ache to tug at her curls and watch her arch for me again, but that ship has sailed.

Being with her is only going to make her a target for my enemies. I've put enough people in danger to last a lifetime.

She is lurking around a destroyed home that contains the symbol of my enemy. I don't know what she is hiding from me, but one way or another I will be getting to the bottom of it.

Her gaze connects with mine and I lurch between the desire to kiss her and kill her.

Knowing that she is somehow connected to the

Domingos cartel could be useful, but based on how resistant she's been in the time that I've known her, I doubt it.

Still, why would she be lurking around a place they've claimed?

What would Carlos have to do with her if she is tied to the Domingos cartel?

None of it makes sense.

I turn away from Hadley, knowing that I can't kill her yet. I need to know what she knows.

"What street are we on?" I start opening the cupboards and looking through them. Though there are a few needles, they could have been left here by anyone who snuck in .

"Hollis." She slams a cupboard shut when I try to open it. "Stop looking through shit and just get out of here."

"Why is it so important to you that I don't know about this place? It just looks like a burned down little home, but you were willing to sneak into it. That seems a little odd to me, don't you think?"

She scowls. "You never would have known about it if you hadn't decided to stalk me here."

"I didn't stalk you here. I simply feared for your safety while feeling suspicious about your intentions."

"Look, why don't we both just leave? You're right. I have no business being here."

I spin around and grab her by the throat gently, pushing her back against a wall. Instead of the fear I expect, I see nothing but excitement shining in her eyes. My cock hardens as she glares at me.

"Get your fucking hands off of me before I break them," she says, her hands coming up to grab mine. She tries to pull my hand away but I keep it in place.

"I don't think you want that. I can see the excitement in

your eyes. I bet if I slipped my hand in those tiny little shorts of yours I would find you soaking wet for me again."

"You're a bastard," she says as I let go of her and take a step back.

"And you're a liar." I hum to myself as I start rummaging through the cupboards again, looking for anything that might tell me who used to live here. "Tell you what, if you don't want to tell me about what is going on in this house, then we can make a deal."

"What kind of deal?"

"I'll give you two hundred dollars to go to dinner with me and tell me what you're doing here."

I keep my back to her, though I'm not sure she isn't going to drive a knife in it the first chance that she gets.

"Two hundred dollars is not enough to put up with you or your prying questions," she says, venom in her voice.

"Three hundred?"

"A thousand."

I chuckle and shake my head. "Now you're just being greedy."

"From what I understand, you have more than enough money to meet my requirements. You want to go to dinner, I want money for school."

I turn around and approach her, getting closer and closer until her back is pressed against one of the charred walls. She looks up at me, and for a brief second, there is fear in her eyes.

Good. At least she knows enough to be afraid.

"If you were smart, you would take me up on my offer instead of trying to make a deal. I know you *think* you want to play with the big boys, but trust me, you really don't."

She glowers up at me. "I would never make the mistake of trusting you."

"Smart girl. I wouldn't do that either. It would be the worst thing you ever did." I take a step away from her, turning away before she sees the way my cock is straining against my pants.

Instead of rummaging through the cupboards, I head for the door. I can come back here and look through the house later, when Hadley isn't around. I want to know why the Domingos' sigil is here and how she is connected.

It would help to have those answers before I have dinner with her. I don't like being the only one left in the dark.

Being left in the dark is how people die.

"Five hundred dollars," I say without looking back at her. "You'll go to dinner with me Thursday night, tell me whatever I want to know, and then I will give you the five hundred dollars."

"Fine."

I smirk as I look over my shoulder at her. "Try to wear something pretty. I don't want people to think I make a habit of hanging around with petty criminals who break into abandoned buildings."

"You're infuriating!" Her voice carries after me as I walk out of the house, amused with the entire situation.

If Hadley thinks that she is calling the shots here, she has another thing coming.

7

HADLEY

As I stand in front of the restaurant Thursday night, I wonder what the hell I'm doing here.

I never should have agreed to tell Jovan anything about my life. His questions are going to dig too deep. He's going to make me uncomfortable and push me because he can. There is no doubt in my mind that he is going to hold the money over my head.

A smarter woman would be running away right now. If I didn't need the money, I wouldn't even entertain the thought of meeting with him.

Well, the money and the way he intrigues me like nobody else ever has. I know that I should stay far away from him. He's a dangerous man and he has the power to do whatever he wants.

That only makes spending time with him that much more exciting.

After taking a deep breath, I walk into the restaurant and feel like I've been transported to another world. Every-thing is sleek, white, and modern. It looks like even touching one of the decorations will make the entire place shatter into a thousand pieces.

The host leads me through the restaurant, around the tables and to the back where there are private rooms. A glass door opens and a waiter steps out. He smiles politely to me and nods to the host before heading in what I assume is the direction of the kitchen.

I wait a moment before walking into the private room. There is a large booth in front of me with white leather and a frosted glass table. The wall to the left of me is a waterfall that cascades down into a small pool.

I don't belong here.

Jovan slides out of the booth, looking like heaven and hell at the same time. His shirt is dark, making his dark eyes pop. His gaze moves up and down my body slowly, lingering where my silver dress hugs my curves.

"You look stunning tonight, Hadley," he says, his tone as sweet as honey, though the look in his eyes is anything but.

"Thank you," I say, taking a seat on the opposite side. The leather is like butter against my skin as I sit down.

Jovan takes his seat as the host produces two menus from somewhere else in the room. After giving us the menus, the host disappears through the doors.

"You really do look good tonight, Hadley. I almost didn't recognize you as the criminal breaking into houses."

I roll my eyes and open the menu. "I'm not the criminal here."

"You really should watch that tongue of yours. It's going to get you in trouble one day." Jovan smirks and leans back in his seat. "If you like lobster, the bisque is amazing."

"I'm more of a burger kind of girl," I say, flipping to the burger section of the menu.

As I search for something not covered in truffle oil or gold, Jovan grabs a remote and starts playing with the color of the lights overhead. He finally settles on a dark blue tone that shifts to a slightly lighter one every several seconds.

"Do I even want to know how much this dinner is going to cost?" I ask, turning the menu around and holding it out to him. "There aren't any prices."

Jovan shrugs and fiddles with another remote until soft instrumental music starts playing. "I wouldn't bother with worrying about the cost. I'm paying for dinner."

I turn the menu back around and start scanning through the burgers again. My heart is racing a mile a minute as I look through the options for dinner. Finally, I find one that sounds like something I might enjoy.

Most of my food is limited to the few meals I know how to make at home and whatever I can get at a fast food place.

The waiter appears with a bottle of wine and pours our glasses before taking our orders. As soon as the door is shut behind the waiter, Jovan turns to me with a look that sends a shiver down my spine.

"Now, I have some questions for you," he says, picking up the napkin and pulling off the silver band that holds it together.

He twirls the silver band on the table, studying me. The corner of his mouth tilts upward.

"What do you want to talk about?" I ask, feigning ignorance as I reach for my water. I take a sip and stare at him over the edge of the glass.

"Hadley, you're a smarter woman than that." He stops spinning the band. "Why don't we start with something simple?"

"That really depends on your definition of simple."

He chuckles and shakes his head. "Alright, if that's how you want to play, then I'm game. Tell me about your childhood."

"You call that simple?" I scoff and lean back in my seat. I cross my arms and wait for him to say something else but he keeps his mouth shut.

That infuriating smirk makes me crazy. I don't know whether I want to kiss him or kill him.

"There's not much to talk about. My childhood was shit but it made me into who I am."

Jovan arches an eyebrow. "You're going to have to explain that one a little more."

"Nope. There is no way that I'm going to start unpacking my childhood trauma with you. I don't see how it's relevant to anything you want to know."

The waiter walks into the room and puts our appetizers in front of us. The crab dip in front of me is mouthwatering. I grab one of the little crackers and scoop up some of the dip before popping it into my mouth.

"This is amazing," I say as the waiter pours Jovan a glass of wine. When the waiter holds the bottle out to me, I shake my head. "No, thank you."

"Not much of a drinker?" Jovan asks as the waiter leaves the room.

"Like I said, shitty childhood influenced the person I am now."

"So, you never drink?"

I shrug. "I didn't say that. I just agreed that I'm not much of a drinker. Every now and then I'll have a glass of wine, but that's about it."

"Alright, so, why were you in that house?"

I eat some more of the crab dip, stalling for time. When he arches an eyebrow and starts spinning the band again, I know he is getting impatient.

I can't decide if I'm happy that I'm pushing his buttons just as much as he is pushing mine. He needs to understand he doesn't control me, even if I do need his money.

Besides, riling him up is part of my fun.

There's something about seeing him lose even an inch of control that sends a wave of lust rolling through my body. I want to see him that out of control with me pinned against the wall as he drives into me.

"Whatever is going through your head right now makes me think that you are up to no good," Jovan says, his voice soft and sultry as he leans across the table.

"I thought you said I couldn't play with the big boys?" I smile sweetly at him and sit forward, my face inches from his. "Wouldn't that mean that I'm only up to good?"

"Stop dodging the question, Hadley. What were you doing in that house?"

I arch an eyebrow at the frustration in his tone. "Why does it matter to you? You seem to be very interested in that house."

He exhales hard, his hand curling into a fist before relaxing. "Do I need to remind you that the five hundred dollars is contingent on you cooperating with me?"

I swallow hard and bite my tongue as the waiter comes back into the room with our food. I don't bother to touch my burger as I stare at Jovan, considering how much I should tell him.

If he digs deep enough or asks Carlos about me, he is going to have the entire story. It's better that I tell him what I want him to know than allowing him to rummage through my life.

"I used to live there before my parents died," I say, not volunteering the reason why I visit the house. I don't need him to know that I miss the house where my life was ruined over and over again.

"Alright, so you used to live there. That still doesn't tell me why you would be going to a burned and abandoned house after work."

I shrug and pick up my burger, picking a big bite as I try to think of a reason that he won't see through immediately.

"I went there because I was thinking about finally burning it to the ground."

He sighs and breaks one of the crab legs in front of him before dipping it into the hot honey butter. Jovan sucks the meat from the leg, clearly waiting for me to elaborate. When I don't, his eyes narrow.

"Hadley, you're not playing the game properly. Normal people like you don't wake up one morning with a desire to burn things to the ground."

"To be fair, I had just finished work. That means that I had already been up for the whole day. That's plenty of time to consider arson."

Surprisingly, he laughs as I take another big bite of my burger. Jovan shakes his head and eats another crab leg before wiping his fingers on the napkin. When he crosses his arms, it feels like my stomach drops out of my body.

It feels like he can see through me. Sitting across from him and seeing that stern look on his face makes me think that he already knows everything he could ever need to know about me.

Though I know it's not true, it makes me uncomfortable.

"Fine, you don't want to tell me more about your child-hood than that. I can accept that for now."

"Can you?"

He shrugs. "Tell me why you're willing to do all this for money. You're bending to my whims but you've clearly got a backbone. I think you might be one of the most stubborn people that I have ever met."

"Thank you."

Jovan rolls his eyes. "That's not a compliment, Hadley."

"Sure sounded like one to me."

I finish off my burger as he shakes his head and takes a sip of his wine. Jovan continues to eat, but he never looks away from me for long.

"You know, if you keep staring at me like that, you might just burn a hole through my body."

He smirks and finishes his food. "You didn't answer my question."

"I need the money for school."

Jovan scoffs. "It's more than that. You say that it's for school but you get this strange look on your face when you talk about it. That's what tells me that it's more than just needing money for school."

"I told you. I had a shit childhood. I'm going to school to become a kindergarten teacher."

"You want to work with people who are still pissing themselves?" He chuckles and sips his wine. "You know, you could do that in a nursing home and make a lot more money."

"It's not just about that."

"Then explain it to me so I understand."

I fiddle with one of the rings on my fingers, twisting it around and around as I look at the waterfall behind him. The blue lights are making the water look magical as it flows down the white stone wall.

"Teachers have the power to make a difference in a child's life. If I had a teacher who cared enough to step into my life when I started going to school, things might have turned out differently for me."

He nods for a moment and finishes his glass of wine. "You don't seem like you're going to tell me more than that."

"To be honest, I don't know why you would want to know more than that."

Jovan gives me a smile that makes my heart skip a beat. "You're not like anyone else that I've ever met."

"That sounded like a normal person's response," I say as the waiter enters the room.

Jovan pulls out his card and hands it to the waiter. The waiter takes off with the card, leaving us alone again. As I watch him eat the last of the crab dip, I wonder if there's more to Jovan than the life he's crafted for himself.

When the waiter comes back with the card, Jovan gets up from the table and comes around to my side. He holds out his hand, waiting for me to take it.

Something shifts between us the moment I take his hand. I don't know what it is, but it feels like I can't turn back from whatever it is we've just started.

Jovan leads me out of the restaurant, his hand still wrapped around mine. My mind is racing a mile a minute, trying to figure out why he is acting this way and what he has to gain from it. None of this is making sense to me at all, though I desperately want it to.

He walks with me to my car, not prying for any other information. It's only once we stop beside the car that he finally looks at me with that amused smile on his face.

"You know the other benefit to getting to know people is knowing how to destroy them," Jovan says, leaning closer to me.

He stands in front of me, close enough that our chests are nearly touching. My breath hitches as he lowers his head, kissing me in a way that sets my nerves on fire.

When Jovan pulls away, my mind is reeling. I don't know what this means or why he kissed me. I sure as hell don't know why I let him. When he leaned in, I should have pushed him away and told him to get lost.

"Get home safely," he says before turning and walking away.

I watch as he fades into the distance before turning and getting in my car. As I sit there, staring at the wheel, I know that I'm already in too deep.

Jovan has this way about him that draws me in and excites me. He's like the high that my parents chased for years.

I need to stay as far away from him as possible.

8

JOVAN

"IT'S A GOOD DAY FOR SAILING," RIO SAYS EARLY Sunday morning as I jump from the dock onto the small speedboat. "The delivery is about a half hour out. They're waiting for the inspection before they bring it in."

I nod and take my seat behind the wheel as Rio unties the boat from the dock. I rev the engine to life and we take off out of the marina. Rio takes the seat beside me, checking over his gun as we leave Miami behind.

"So," Rio says, drawing out the word as he looks at me. I can feel his gaze burning into the side of my head and it unnerves me. "You want to talk about why you took the new bottle service girl to dinner the other night?"

"How the hell do you know about that?"

Rio chuckles. "You went to a restaurant with her. Are you expecting that to be kept quiet? Kennedy has a big mouth."

"Your girlfriend needs to keep her nose out of my business." I glance over at Rio in time to see his smile drop.

"You try telling her that." Rio scowls at me before he

relaxes and chuckles. "I'll talk to her but I'm sure she is going to have a few choice words to say about it."

"At least if your body turns up, I know who to go after," I say, my tone teasing. "Although, if you don't handle her big mouth, I may have to."

Rio's smile falters. "You know, if you ever do anything to Kennedy, I'll be forced to get involved."

"I know, so the message better come across and we don't have to worry about that, huh?"

His loyalty may be to my cartel, but it is always to Kennedy first. I knew that when he became my right hand man and I've never asked him to change that.

Even if it drives me insane, his dedication to her has never compromised his loyalty to me.

"Hadley talked to Kennedy about our dinner, then?" I ask, changing the subject slightly.

Rio nods and flicks the safety on the gun, tucking it into his holster. "Yeah. Hadley came over last night. I was told to keep my ass in the bedroom while they did their girly shit."

Now, that's interesting.

If Hadley was telling people about our night together, I either pissed her off or scared her more than I thought I did.

"You know, you get this look on your face when Hadley is brought up," Rio says, smirking as he goes to the front of the boat and takes a seat, staring out at the waves. "It's almost like there's a human living inside of you instead of a robot."

"Funny," I say, sarcasm dripping from my tone. "Any more bits of wisdom that you would like to share?"

"I would say that you should do a good job of not pissing Hadley off since she's the only woman that seems to be tolerating you."

"Too late for that," I say, smirking slightly. "I don't think we've had a conversation where I haven't pissed her off. I doubt that day will ever come."

"It'll happen if you want it to happen."

A white boat appears as a small dot on the horizon. I head for it as Rio grabs the binoculars and watches the boat.

The boat is rocking with the waves, sending us lurching to the side slightly. Clouds are starting to drift across the blue sky as we pull alongside the boat. Rio and the man on the other boat tie both boats together. I kill the engine once we're secured and board the sailing yacht with Rio.

The men lead the way down into the sailing yacht and to one of the cupboards in the bedroom. The man pops the cupboard and a hidden passage opens up. We climb down the ladder into a massive holding space.

Pallets of white bricks wrapped in layers of plastic sit in the middle of the holding area. When I look at the product, all I can see is dollar signs.

"Alright, boys," I say as I approach the first pallet. "Inspection time."

THE SUN IS HIGH IN THE SKY BY THE TIME WE GET BACK to the marina. Rio docks the boat and ties it off before taking a seat. He reaches into a cooler and pulls out a couple beers, tossing one to me before cracking open his own.

"I got news from one of the guys down in the warehouse district that Felix has been spotted going into one of them," Rio says after I've taken my first sip of beer. "There've been three visits in the past week."

My hand tightens around the can and I take another sip, trying to control my temper.

"Felix Domingos is a dead man," I say once I feel like I

can talk without screaming. "There is no way that he is going to be able to come back here and lay claim to Miami."

Rio nods and downs half his beer. "He's been seen at the family's old estate too. Someone said he was searching through the rubble but I don't know what he would have been trying to find. Most of what was there is now long gone."

"It should be. I poured more than enough gasoline through that fucking house to get it to burn to the ground."

I finish my beer and get up to grab a second can. If Felix is lurking around a warehouse and his family home, then he is looking for something. The people I have following him aren't doing a good enough job if they haven't figured out what yet.

I'm going to have to give them a reminder of what their job is.

"Who do we have that can find out what he's looking for without alerting him to what they're going?" I ask, cracking open the drink.

"We could send Giana in deeper. Have her spend more time with him. Maybe get to know him at the club. I was speaking to her yesterday and she said that he's been coming to see her dance every other night."

"Why the hell is someone who should be hiding this visible? It doesn't make sense." I shake my head and look up at the sky. "What game do you think he's playing?"

"Intimidation tactic. He wouldn't be lurking around Miami if he didn't have someone backing him."

I run a hand down my face before sitting up straighter. "Alessio is running Atlanta right now. He might know something. He used to back the Domingos family back in the day."

"If anybody is going to know what Felix is up to, it's probably going to be him."

Getting in contact with Alessio is the last thing I want to do. He's just returned home to deal with members of his mafia that keep stepping out of line. He's got more on his plate than I do at the moment. But he has spies everywhere. If something is going on, he knows it and he could help. His mafia is nearly three times the size of my cartel.

"Alessio probably isn't going to be able to get involved with this," Rio says as he finishes his own drink. "He's your ally and a friend, but you know that he is dealing with other problems. Besides, Felix would know that you're working with the Marchetti mafia now that Alessio is at the helm."

"I know that, but there is nothing that I can do about it. He is the only one who might have some information I can trust. I need every advantage I can get if Felix is going to try and take Miami back."

"Your decision, but I think if you give your people a little more time, they might be able to come up with the same information that Alessio is going to give you. He may not have the time to deal with this right now."

I pull out my phone. "He's a good friend. If anyone is going to come through, it's going to be him."

My stomach lurches as I scroll through my contacts, looking for Alessio's number. When I find it, I hit the call button and wait while the phone rings. With each ring, I feel like calling him is even more of a bad idea.

If I were a better friend, I would leave him alone to deal with his problems in peace — step in to help him if needed. However, I'm not asking him to take time away from dealing with a potential uprising to help me.

I've never felt like more of a worse friend but I need to think about my people. Protecting them is my top priority.

I need to know what Felix is up to.

"Hey, Jovan," Alessio says when the call connects. "This is kind of a bad time, as I'm sure you are aware."

Alessio isn't the easiest man to deal with, grumpy as fuck when things go his way, hell on earth when things go sideways, so I know what I'm getting into, but he is the only one I know who might be able to help with my Felix problem.

"Yeah, I know. I'm sorry, man, but I need your help with Felix. I want to get out ahead of this before it becomes a problem. Do you know why he has decided to return to Miami?"

"If we are going to talk about the Domingos cartel, I would like to do so in person."

"Name the time and the place," I say, relief coloring my voice.

"I'm going to be in Miami on the twentieth. If you want to discuss Felix, then we can set up a meeting."

"Alright. Send me a message with the details and I'll meet you there."

"Will do." He hangs up, as I finish my second beer. Rio looks at me.

"Well, that sounded like it went well," Rio states.

"He's coming back soon and we'll meet with him then. I know he's dealing with his own shit, so I'm grateful he is willing to take the time to help us."

"When's that?"

"In three weeks. Our people have until then to get me some useful information. If Alessio gets more information than our people do, I'm going to have to reconsider how lenient I have been. Alessio may be having problems with his people, but I doubt that he will be having them for long."

I jump down onto the dock. "Get home to your girlfriend. I have some other things that I need to take care of tonight."

Rio chuckles and wiggles his eyebrow at me. "Going to go see Hadley?"

"Fuck off." I head down the dock, not wanting to talk about Hadley anymore.

The only thing I'm going home to is a cold shower so I can fuck my fist for the hundredth time while thinking about her.

9

HADLEY

Kennedy grins as she leans back on the couch and kicks her feet up on the coffee table late one night after a particularly long shift.

"You know, I don't know if going back to that club for my shift tomorrow is a good idea," she says as she relaxes into the cushions. "I keep thinking about leaving. Rio has offered to support us both."

"What does Rio do?" I ask. I take a long sip on my milkshake as I curl up on the opposite end of her couch.

Kennedy's face pales slightly but she shrugs it off. "He's Jovan's enforcer. Right hand man. Whatever you want to call it."

For a moment, I wonder if she knows what Jovan really does for a living. When she gives me a sheepish smile, it's clear that she knows.

I thought she would have been smart enough to stay away from the cartel shit. But even as I think it, I know that I'm a massive hypocrite. After everything with my drug-addicted parents, I'm still willing to toe the line of being wrapped up in cartel business.

Although, I didn't know that I was walking into a cartel-owned business when I applied for the job. I had heard rumors, but powerful criminals owning clubs in Miami is common.

It's expected.

I've spent my entire life around the darkness that comes with the cartel controlling a city. My parents were so deep in the drugs that I started taking care of myself as soon as I could.

It was inevitable that I would end up brushing elbows with the cartel again, even though I've done everything in my power to avoid it.

Kennedy didn't seem like the type, though. She is sweet and bubbly. She doesn't seem like the kind of woman who would get involved with the cartel.

Yet, if there's anything that working at The Brazen has taught me, it's that looks can be deceiving.

Even when I was over a few nights ago and saw Rio, he didn't seem like the kind of man who is in a cartel. He had smiled politely and offered to order dinner before slinking away to their bedroom to hide for the night.

Nothing about him screamed *can kill me with his bare hands and not think twice about it.*

My stomach tosses and turns as I look at her, my eyebrows shooting up my forehead. "Are you sure that it's a good idea to get wrapped up with a member of the cartel like that?"

"Rio and I knew each other before he was ever involved in that stuff. We used to date in high school and then broke up for a few years. I was having some trouble a while back and we ended up moving in together. After that, everything just sort of fell in place."

"Well," I say, swallowing my judgment and smiling. "I

guess that when you're meant to be with someone, you just find your way back to each other sooner or later."

Kennedy beams and nods. "For a long time after we broke up, I couldn't see myself with anybody other than him. He was my first love. Getting our second chance was great."

"How do you handle him working for the cartel?" I put my milkshake on the table and twist to lean against the arm of the couch and face her. "I would be scared shitless to know that my man was out there and willing to die for some dictator."

"I don't think Jovan is a dictator. You just don't like him that much because you are two of the most stubborn people I've ever met." Kennedy laughs and reaches out to pat my leg. "You two just need to fuck and get it out of your system."

My cheeks flame as I glance away from her.

"You didn't!" Kennedy squeals and lunges across the couch at me. She kneels on the cushion in front of me, practically bouncing up and down. "You did!"

"You can't tell anybody."

She shakes her head. "I'm going to have to tell Rio. He can keep a secret, though. Don't worry. He knows that the sex stops if he starts spreading my gossip around."

I laugh and shake my head. "Alright, fine. You can tell Rio."

"I need all of the details. Was it big? You have to tell me if it was big. Personally, I think he's overcompensating for something."

My cheeks burn hotter as I bury my face in my hands. "We are not talking about how big our boss's dick is. Not happening. What would your boyfriend think?"

Kennedy cackles as she pries my hands away from my

face. "Who cares what Rio thinks? He's probably seen the dick hundreds of times. I need to find out if my boyfriend isn't telling me about all the tiny penises he sees."

I laugh so hard tears are streaming down my face. "You're insane."

"Made you feel a little less embarrassed." Kennedy grins from ear to ear. "I'm serious, though. I want all the details of your torrid affair. You can't leave anything out."

"I'm definitely not telling you the details. I've already told you too much. I wasn't supposed to talk about it with anyone."

Kennedy rolls her eyes as she sits back down on the couch. "I'm not just anyone. I happen to be your best friend. You're holding out vital information on me and I need to know."

"There is nothing that you need to know about it. We had one uneventful night before I even knew he was my boss." I narrow my eyes playfully at her. "I still haven't forgiven you for not telling me who I was serving."

Kennedy grins and reaches forward to grab her milkshake off the table. "If I had told you who you were serving, you would have been a lot more nervous."

"I would argue that I would have spilled the bottle either way. I was set up to fail from the beginning." I shake my head and look at her, grinning as the front door opens and Rio walks in. "Those damn heels were hell to walk in."

Rio chuckles and shifts around the bags of groceries he's holding as he walks to the kitchen. "Why is it that I keep coming home only to find you here? You should be off doing something else."

"Like what?"

"I don't know. Maybe making another friend."

I flip him off before getting up and grabbing my drink.

"I do have to get going, actually. There's dying plants to not water and a movie I've been looking forward to watching."

"You just want to avoid talking about the tiny penis," Kennedy says as she gets up and walks me to the door.

"Well, at least I know you're not talking about me," Rio says, laughing when Kennedy rolls her eyes and holds up her finger and her thumb. She pinches them together, leaving only a tiny space between the two.

"You're lucky if it's this big," she says as I slide on my shoes. As I open the door, Kennedy turns her attention to me. "Text me when you get home to let me know you got there safely."

"Will do. Have a good night."

"I will. We're going to be gossiping all about the night you had." Kennedy blows me a kiss before shutting the door behind me.

At least something good came out of working at The Brazen.

WHEN I GET HOME, I RUMMAGE THROUGH THE leftovers in my fridge, looking for the burgers that I had made the night before. My stomach growls as I dig them out along with some strips of bacon.

As I put the food on a plate and pop it into the microwave I hum to myself. Once the microwave is going, I type out a quick message to Kennedy only to get an eggplant emoji with a question mark back. Laughing, I put my phone away and head into the living room to pick my movie for the night.

When I sit down to eat, my stomach lurches. I look down at the plate of food and taste bile. Everything about the leftover burgers seems unappetizing. The longer I look at it, the more I want to throw up.

It's just a burger, Hadley. Stop being a baby and eat your dinner.

The second that I take a bite, my stomach feels like it's been flipped inside out. I get up and race to the bathroom, immediately throwing up everything I just tried to eat.

As I lean against the bathtub, my heart is racing. I still feel like I'm going to be sick.

I try to think back to what could have triggered my stomach trying to claw its way out of my body, but I haven't eaten anything unusual in the last few days. The leftovers I tried to eat are still good.

Maybe it's just PMS.

No sooner does the thought cross my mind than I start doing the math. I met Jovan and slept with him not that long ago. My last period was... When was it? Have I had my period since meeting Jovan?

'Fuck," I say as I haul myself off the floor and wash my mouth out. "There is no way that this is happening. Not a fucking chance that this is happening to me right now. I don't have the time to deal with this."

I head into the kitchen and grab my phone. It only takes a few minutes to order the pregnancy tests.

As I wait for the tests to arrive, I pace around my apartment. Even though I'm trying to stay calm, it feels like the entire world is collapsing around me. I never thought that I would get pregnant from a one night stand. I thought that when I was ready to have children, it would be a conscious choice and not one that was made for me.

I don't know I'm pregnant until I take the test. There's no point worrying about having children until then.

A few minutes later, my phone starts ringing. I answer the call and press the button to buzz in the delivery guy.

The second he knocks on my door, my pulse pounds and my palms grow sweaty. I don't know how the hell I'm going to finish my last year of university with a child.

Hundreds of other women do it every year. You can do it too. All you need to do is take the test and find out if you're having a baby or not.

When I open the door, the delivery man is already gone. I pick up the small brown paper bag and take it inside, my hands shaking. As I open the bag, my chest constricts.

I pull out the tests I ordered and go to the washroom.

Three minutes later, I'm staring at three positive pregnancy tests.

There is no way that I'm telling Jovan about the baby. Our child is not going to be wrapped up in the cartel life.

10

JOVAN

Calling Hadley to my office in the middle of her shift might not be the right move, but I'm tired of watching men flirt with her on the cameras. I sigh and stare at the feed as she weaves through the dancing bodies to make her way to me.

Though I know I should have killed my interest in her, I can't help it.

Secrets shroud her and keep her hidden from the world. I've heard the way she talks to the other employees when things get a little too personal. She detaches herself from them and finds any excuse she can to leave.

Everything personal, she avoids.

I want to know why.

Although, that isn't the only reason why I want to see her more. I can't get the night we spent together out of my head. Each time I think about it, equal parts lust and guilt run through me.

I was such a bastard to her that night but there was nothing else I could do. She was playing with fire and I had been more than happy to burn her. And then there was that situation during the gala. Fuck.

As she moves to another part of the club, a man steps in front of her and says something. Hadley's face darkens for a brief second before she plasters on her charming smile and steps away from him.

The man reaches out and smacks her ass. Before she can turn on him, one of the men who work security for the club steps in. He escorts the man out of the club without so much as a slight hesitation.

If there is one thing I don't tolerate at my clubs, it's people harassing the staff.

The man who slapped Hadley's ass the first night she worked had learned that quickly. I found him the next day and broke his hand.

Nobody puts their hands on her except me.

When the door opens, she smiles and steps inside. The second the door is shut behind her, the smile drops from her face. She looks like I've just kicked her favorite puppy.

"Hadley, good that you could step in here to see me. I was thinking that it's time we talk about what else I require of you," I say, crossing my arms and leaning back in my seat.

She stands a little taller and her eyes narrow, but she keeps her mouth shut. For a moment, I'm disappointed. I like when she runs her mouth, even though I know it's going to get her in all kinds of trouble one of these days.

"I have a meeting in a few weeks. I need you to be there."

"Why?" she asks, a bit of an edge to her voice as she leans back against the door.

"Because I'm telling you."

She shakes her head, her frown deepening. "You really are a pain in my ass sometimes."

"Is that any way to talk to your boss?"

Hadley shrugs. "The way I see it, you could fire me. But I also have a great case for harassment. The last thing you need is media attention drawn to you."

I scowl and consider firing her then and there. My life would be easier without her around. If she was gone, I wouldn't sit in my office and fight temptation every shift she worked.

"The way I see it, I am a threat to you. At least I can be if you push me too far."

"You do know who you're threatening, right?" I arch an eyebrow, my jaw clenching. "I could kill you right now if I wanted to and nobody would care. They would dispose of the body without a second thought."

"If you were going to kill me, you would have done it by now. So, why don't you tell me what I'm doing here and then we can both move on with our nights?"

"Like I said." I exhale hard and try to maintain my composure. Hadley is exceptionally good at getting beneath my skin. "I have a meeting in three weeks and I want you there with me."

"Why me? Why not take Rio? I'm not your bodyguard." Hadley smirks and stands up straight, her hand on the door-knob. "I didn't sign up to get even more involved with the cartel than I already am. You're going to have to find somebody else."

"Hadley, you seem to forget that you agreed to be my bottle service girl at every meeting I take."

She sighs, her shoulders slumping slightly. "Alright. Just tell me when and where. I'll be there."

My mouth nearly drops open as I look at her. Not once has she ever agreed to anything this quickly.

"Are you feeling alright?" I ask as I get up and round the desk. "Being this agreeable isn't like you."

Hadley scowls and crosses her arms. "Look, I made a deal with you and I'm going to stick to that deal. Pretty soon I'll be done with this job and on my way. I just have to get through the next several weeks and then I can go back to school and the life I had before I met you."

I chuckle, though her words sting slightly. Though I know that I am by no means her favorite person, I thought that she was starting to warm up to me.

Perhaps I only have myself fooled.

It's better if she leaves. People you get attached to only die in the end. You don't need to lose another person.

It's better to be alone than to live with the grief of losing another person.

"Hadley, there is no more life before you met me. You work for the cartel now. You're in just as deep as the rest of us, whether you like it or not."

Her cheeks turn a bright shade of red and anger blazes in her eyes.

There's that passion I'm looking for.

"I'm *not* part of the cartel," she says, indignation in her tone. "I would *never* sink that low."

I grin as I stalk toward her like a predator hunting their prey. Her breath hitches as I loom over her, our bodies nearly pressed together. As I run one finger along the curve of her cheek, I'm sure that she's going to start yelling.

Instead, lust fills her gaze, though I can see her internal fight over it. Her stare is conflicted. Hadley looks like a deer caught in the headlights without an escape.

"Darling, you sunk that low when you put my cock in your pretty little pussy. Now, if you would like to reconsider your position on how low you have to sink, I would be more than happy to hear it. I don't take too kindly to people insulting my profession."

She bites her bottom lip for a second. The urge to take that bottom lip between my own teeth before kissing her senseless is strong. I want to taste every inch of her.

"I stand by what I said," she says, placing her hands on my chest and trying to push me back a step. "Would you get out of my fucking bubble? You make it impossible to think when you're acting like that."

"Acting like what?" I ask, my tone innocent as I smile at her.

"You have got to be the most irritating person that I have ever met. I have no clue how you managed to take control of an entire city when it seems like the only thing you know how to do with any skill is piss people off."

I grin and shrug. "I don't know. You seemed to think that I was pretty skilled with my fingers when you were coming all over them."

Hadley's cheeks seem impossibly red as she shakes her head. "Is this really the kind of thing we should be talking about at work?"

"Now seems as good a time as any."

"You're only doing this to get a reaction out of me." She opens the door and glares at me. "I'll go to the meeting with you but I'm not going to stay in this office and let you talk to me this way."

"Be honest with yourself for once, Hadley." I step closer to her and reach around to slam the door shut. Thankfully, the club is loud and I'm sure that nobody heard it. I don't need someone investigating the situation.

"I *am* honest with myself."

"I don't think you are." I dip my head to trail my lips along her collarbone, grazing the sensitive skin with my teeth. "If you were being honest with yourself, you would admit how turned on you are right now. You would admit that you're soaking wet because the things I say to you make you want me more."

"I want you like I want to roll around naked in a patch of poison ivy."

"That can be arranged."

She sighs and runs a hand down her face. "I already told you that I would go to this meeting with you. What more could you possibly want from me tonight? I'm really not in the mood to keep playing these games."

The shift in her tone has me backing off. I study her for a minute, trying to figure out what's wrong with her. However, the more I look, the clearer it is that her face is a mask entirely void of emotion. If she doesn't want to let someone in, they aren't getting in.

Behind it all, I can see the broken little girl still lingering there.

I don't know what happened to her when she was little, but she has admitted to trauma of some kind.

I'm going to find out who hurt her and then I'm going to make them pay.

"You should go home and get some rest if you are feeling unwell. If you want to go, I can have someone else cover your tables."

"I'm not going to lose out on the tips just because I feel like shit." Hadley plasters on a fake smile and opens the door. "I'm going to go back out there and do my job. Just text me all the details about the meeting. I assume you have my number or can get it from my file."

"I can." I sigh and walk over to the door, holding it open for her. "I'm going to pay you extra for this meeting but I want to train you in self-defense. The man we're going to be meeting is a friend, but there are a lot of dangerous people out there and you need to know how to take care of yourself."

"Alright," she says with a slight nod. "Send me those details too. A few shooting lessons isn't the worst idea unless you're worried about me shooting you in the head."

"Well, I wasn't worried about that before, but I might be now," I say, my tone teasing as she tries to smother the first sign of a smile that she's had all evening. "Have a good night, Hadley."

"Good night, Mr. Aguilar," she says as a waiter walks by.

I close the door behind her and wait a moment before returning to the screens with the camera feeds. Hadley walks over to Kennedy and whispers something in her ear before heading back to her table.

As I settle in for the rest of the night, I wonder what's bothering her. In the weeks that I've known and bothered her, I've never seen her look that defeated.

Stop caring about her. Caring about her is going to get her killed. You can't afford to lose another person. Losing your family nearly ruined you. Losing her would destroy you entirely. Walk away from her now, while you still can.

Though I know the little voice in my head is right, I can't tear my eyes away from the screen.

If she is my ruination, then I'm opening my arms and welcoming her into my embrace.

11

HADLEY

I'VE ALWAYS SAID THAT I WOULD NEVER HAVE ANYTHING to do with guns. I didn't want to be like my parents. There is no need for me to be armed at all times, waiting to shoot someone because something they did rubbed me the wrong way.

That's why going to the shooting lesson with Jovan feels so wrong. Learning how to shoot is something I never thought I would do, but after the talk with Jovan in his office where he said I am stuck in the cartel, if I ever want out, it seems that it's become a necessity.

Jovan stands in the parking lot of the shooting range with a giant smile on his face. It's the kind of smile that people wear when they are at peace with everything around them.

I have a very hard time believing that anything about him is at peace.

"Good to see that you did decide to show up," Jovan says as I join him near the doors. "For a day or two I was worried that you were going to bail on me."

"If I have to spend time with you, I may as well know

how to kill you," I say, giving him a sweet smile as he holds the door open for me.

Jovan laughs and shakes his head. "You know what? I'm not even surprised that is your reason for showing up."

"Good. Don't underestimate me, Jovan. It would be a mistake."

He moves closer to me, his hand brushing against mine as he leads the way past the front counter and through a set of doors that lead to a gun room.

"I would never make the mistake of underestimating you, Hadley. I've known too many women who look as sweet as you but would kill me in the blink of an eye."

Jovan starts to look through the guns, talking to the man in the room about several of them. I barely pay attention as I look around. There is something thrilling about knowing how to defend myself, even if guns aren't my weapon of choice.

My baby has a cartel leader for a father. I'm not naive enough to think that the dangers of the cartel won't bleed into our lives eventually. I want to be able to defend myself and my child when the worst happens.

As far as I could find through searching the internet, my baby is the only heir to the Aguilar cartel. I know how much heirs mean to people like Jovan.

Hopefully, I'll be done working at the club before I start to show. He won't ever have to know that the baby exists.

However, I know that it's not going to stay a secret for long after I start showing. Rio will find out through Kennedy. I'm sure that he will run to his boss as soon as he can to tell him about the child.

"Alright, let's go shoot," Jovan says, handing me a gun and grinning. "Keep that pointed at the ground and unloaded unless you are planning on shooting it. I don't want to take a bullet to the back."

"Only cowards shoot someone from point blank in the back," I say as I follow him through a set of swinging doors to the range.

There are several little booths in a row with targets far down on another wall. Jovan leads the way to one of the little booths and puts his gun down on the counter that runs the length of the booth.

"First, you're going to want to wear ear protection," he says, picking up the ear muffs and holding them over my ears. "I'm going to shoot a few and then we're going to put a new target up and you're going to shoot."

Jovan adjusts my ear muffs before putting on his own, then loading his gun. I watch him flick off the safety and cock the gun before aiming it at the target downrange. Jovan's finger curls around the trigger as his other hand supports the gun.

He fires shot after shot, each one a loud crack in the air. Though it's muffled by the ear muffs, the shots are still loud.

Jovan stops shooting and unloads the gun before putting it back down on the counter. He presses a little button that brings the target zipping over to us.

All of his shots have landed either in the center of the target body or in the head.

"We want to make sure that you can kill someone if you have to," Jovan says as he puts his target to the side and hangs another. He pushes a button that sends the target a short distance down the range. "We'll start close and move it farther back, the better you get."

"You really think that I'm going to need to kill some-one?" I ask as he shows me how to load the gun.

Jovan shrugs and steps behind me, putting the gun in

my hands. "You're going to flick off the safety and then cock the gun. You want to support the gun with one hand while your other holds it."

"People in movies only use one hand," I say as his hands cover my own and he shows me how to hold the gun.

A shiver runs down my spine as his chest presses against my back. The warmth of his body pressing against mine makes heat rushes straight to my core. The spicy scent of his cologne wraps around me as Jovan guides my body into the right position.

"They do, and their shots go wild. There are going to be times when you can only use one hand, but you need to be a good shot to do that first. Becoming a good shot means learning to shoot the right way."

My stomach lurches as he has me flick off the safety and cock the gun. I didn't want to ever have to learn how to shoot someone. This isn't the kind of life that I've wanted for myself.

I'm supposed to be a teacher. I should be working on lesson plans to showcase in my portfolio for school. Or I could be picking up more hours at the club and getting rent money for when I'm in school and can't work as much.

"Don't put your finger on the trigger unless you're sure that you're going to shoot," he says. His breath on the back of my neck makes me feel weak in the knees, reminding me I need to put as much distance between us as possible.

"You want to take a step back?"

Jovan chuckles, taking my earlobe between his teeth gently. "Nervous, Hadley?"

"I thought we were here to shoot."

"Then shoot. Look at where you want the bullet to go and then squeeze the trigger."

His hands are still over mine as he helps me aim. Jovan's

finger squeezes mine and the bullet whizzes through the target.

"I did it," I say, looking over my shoulder at him. "I hit the target!"

He laughs, his smile sending a million butterflies rapidly beating against my stomach. "You did hit it. Now, do that a couple dozen more times."

I take a deep breath as he steps back and shoot on my own. While the bullet doesn't hit the center of the target like it did before, I still manage to hit the outline of the person.

Jovan's body is still close to mine. I can feel his eyes burning a hole in my back. I feel like I'm going to combust when he's this close to me.

Only a little bit longer and then I can go home and try to forget that this day ever happened.

After I finish the magazine, Jovan pulls the target back in. Most of the shots have hit the paper in some way or another, though most of them have left holes in non-critical places.

"Not bad," Jovan says as he sets the target to the side with his. "What do you say we head out of here and I buy some lunch?"

I should tell him no. I should insist that I'm going to go home without him. If he comes home with me, I know there is no way that I'm going to be able to resist him for long.

Not when he's looking at me like he is going to devour me the first chance he gets.

"Lunch sounds good," I say, taking a step back from him.

Jovan takes the gun from me and disassembles it. After we return the guns and sign out, Jovan leads the way to his car.

It's not one I've seen before. The car he's driving today is vintage with cream leather and a black body. My mouth drops open at the look of the car.

"You really do have a lot of money," I say as he pops the trunk and tosses my target in. "That's a gorgeous car. I didn't think a man like you would be interested in classic cars."

Jovan smiles and closes the trunk. "You don't seem like the kind of person who would be interested in cars either."

"I have a friend who restored them during summers throughout high school. I helped him and he gave me enough money to keep me afloat during my first year of university."

"One of these days you're going to have to tell me more about your life. It seems like there is still a lot I don't know about you."

"There's plenty you don't know about me." I pull my hair back from my face and put it up into a messy bun. "What do you want to do for lunch? My car's here but we can meet somewhere."

He studies me for a moment before tossing me the keys to his car. I barely catch them, my eyes widening as I look at him.

"Tell you what, we can take my car and pick yours up later. You can drive."

"You're kidding!" I say, my voice rising an octave as I look at the car.

"Not even a little bit." Jovan heads to the passenger side and gets in. "Come on. I'm craving a burger for lunch."

I can't move fast enough to get in the car and start it up. The engine roars to life as I grip the wheel and grin. It's been a long time since I had a chance to drive a classic car. I'm going to make the most of it.

Jovan reaches over and turns on the radio before leaning back in the seat and rolling his window down.

"Drive for as long as you like. I'll put more gas in it if I need to."

I glance over at him, shocked before I focus on the road again. This isn't the first time that Jovan has surprised me.

I doubt it will be that last.

A FEW HOURS LATER, JOVAN IS STILL LOUNGING ON MY couch and laughing along with a movie we put on while we were eating. He grins as he looks over at me.

It's hard to comprehend the sight in front of me. There is a man who murders people, sells drugs and guns, and who knows what else just sitting on my couch and watching a movie.

"What are we doing here, Jovan?" I ask as I lean back against the arm of the couch and face him.

He grabs the remote and pauses the movie before twisting to face me. "What do you mean?"

"You're sitting here in my living room like we're friends." I try to phrase my sentences carefully because I don't want to seem like an ass. "I appreciate everything that you're doing for me, though you are the one who's dragging me into it in the first place."

Jovan chuckles and shrugs. "Well, you might be right about that. You were the one who didn't want to tuck your tail between your legs and run while you still had the chance."

"I'm not exactly the kind of person who is willing to back down from a challenge." I pull my knees to my chest and wrap my arms around them. "I should have run away, though."

His expression softens slightly as his gaze travels over my body. "Hadley, I wouldn't involve you if I didn't think that I could keep you safe."

"You don't seem like you want to keep me safe. You taught me how to shoot a gun today, Jovan. That doesn't exactly scream safe to me."

"It's as safe as you're going to get in a city like Miami." Jovan grabs my ankle and yanks me across the couch to him.

I fall back into the cushions and he moves to hover over me, one knee between my legs.

"As for what I'm doing here, I happen to like your company, even if you remind me of a coiled cobra sometimes."

My breath hitches as one of his hands lands on my hip. The other is beside my head, keeping him above me. His face lowers until his lips are brushing against mine. As he kisses me, my heart races.

This is a bad idea. I should tell him to go before we take things too far.

His body presses against mine as we kiss, our tongues tangling. Jovan groans and nips my bottom lip before pulling away slightly. His gaze searches mine for a moment.

I don't know what he sees there, but whatever it is brings him back in for another kiss.

My fingers weave through his hair as I pull him closer, enjoying the feeling of his body on mine. As his cock presses against me, my core starts to pulse. I moan into the kiss, hooking one leg around his hip.

If this is wrong, I don't want to be right.

Staying away from him is impossible. I may as well lean

into the attraction that flows between us and make the most of it.

Jovan rolls his hips and bites my bottom lip as I reach between us. I slide my hands beneath his shirt, feeling his flexing muscles beneath my hands.

"Bedroom," he says, breaking the kiss and standing up. Fire is burning in his eyes as he reaches out a hand to help me up.

As soon as I'm on my feet, he spins me around with him and pins me against the wall. His mouth trails along my neck, biting and sucking a path that drives me wild. My hands roam his body, my fingers digging into his flesh.

Jovan looks at me with hooded eyes as I pull away from him and get to my knees in front of him. He pulls his shirt over his head and tosses it to the side before taking off the rest of his clothing.

His cock bobs in front of me as his hands pull the elastic out of my hair. My waves cascade around me as I lick his cock from base to tip. He lets out a soft hiss as I take him in my mouth and hollow my cheeks.

"Fuck yes, Hadley. Just like that. You're such a good girl when you suck my cock."

I suck him deeper as he pulls my hair back from my face. When he looks at me, I can feel wetness pooling between my legs. I flick my tongue over the head before sliding my mouth down his length as far as I can go. Another hiss leaves him as I graze my teeth along the sensitive skin.

"If you keep doing that, I'm going to come in your mouth." Jovan rocks his hips in time with my sucking, pushing himself deeper.

I moan around his cock, my hands sliding up and down

his thighs. When he pulls himself out of my mouth, his cock is throbbing and my pussy is aching.

"Strip," he says, his commanding tone only turning me on more.

As I stand and shed my clothing, his gaze never leaves my body. His tongue darts out to lick his bottom lip quickly as I unhook my lace bra and drop it to the ground.

"You're fucking perfection," he says, his voice a throaty growl as he advances on me. "I want you to get on that bed and start playing with yourself."

I feel like a woman possessed as I head to the bedroom and get on the bed. While I sit on the edge of the bed and spread my legs, Jovan leans against the wall. He crosses his arms, his muscles bulging.

My gaze is locked on his as I circle my clit with my fingers, picking up the pace when he reaches down and takes his cock in his hand. As I toy with myself, my orgasm building, I watch the way he strokes himself. His grip is firm as he drags it along the length of his cock before swirling his thumb over the head.

I moan, my eyes closing as I near the edge of the orgasm. Before I can get there, Jovan moves my hand out of the way and picks me up. He slams me into the wall beside my bed, keeping my body pinned as he thrusts into me.

He kisses me hard, biting my bottom lip and swirling his tongue against mine. I roll my hips, meeting his thrusts. My inner walls squeeze around him as my fingers dig into his shoulders.

My orgasm comes hard and fast as he slams harder into me. Jovan groans as he starts thrusting slower, his cock filling me as he pushes deeper.

"Fuck, you feel so good wrapped around my cock," he says, his voice raspy as he turns and tosses me onto the bed.

No sooner do I land than he grabs me by the leg and flips me onto my stomach. Jovan's hands move over my ass, massaging the muscles before he grips my hips. He pulls me up, thrusting into me from behind.

His bruising grip sends me over the edge again, wetness coating my thighs as I come. Jovan thrusts harder, holding me back against him. When he stops, still holding me in place, his cock throbs. He rolls his hips slowly, his cock barely moving as he comes.

We fall to the bed in a sweaty tangled heap. When I roll over and look at him, my mind starts spinning out of control. I have no sense of self-preservation when it comes to him.

Jovan grins and gets on top of me, kissing his way down my body. When his tongue slides along my wet slit, I know that it's going to be a long night.

At least I can't get any more pregnant.

12

JOVAN

When I wake up in the morning, I'm in a room I don't recognize fully. I yawn and sit up to stretch, looking around and trying to clear the sleep fog out of my brain.

Hadley snores softly beside me and the day before comes rushing back to me. I grin as I look at her before panic starts to bubble up inside me.

I'm not the kind of man that stays the night with a woman. I either leave right after we're done fucking, or I wait until they fall asleep and then I go.

Staying with Hadley is something that I've never done before.

She sighs and shifts in her sleep, cuddling a pillow closer. The blanket moves and more of her back is exposed.

There is a part of me that wants to curl up in bed beside her but the much larger part knows that it is a bad idea.

Being involved with Hadley is only going to get her in trouble.

Especially with Felix lurking around.

If he suspects that Hadley means something to me — which she doesn't — then she could be killed.

He would hurt her to get to me. I need to distance myself from her as much as possible to make sure that doesn't happen. She may drive me insane but I don't want anything to happen to her.

The best thing would be to get out of this bed. But I don't. I slide down into the bed beside her and pull the blanket up. She shuffles closer to me, moving until her head is on my shoulder. Her auburn hair fans out around her, shining under the soft light that is filtering through the window.

She's beautiful. There is no denying that.

Hadley is intelligent and funny. She challenges me at every turn and it excites me. She has me doing things that I would never do.

This woman is dangerous in a way that she can't even begin to comprehend.

My mind is at war with my body, telling me to get out of bed and go home even as I wrap my arm around her body and hold her close. Hadley's eyelashes flutter against her cheeks but she doesn't open her eyes.

As she sleeps, I stare up at the ceiling. My fingers drift up and down her spine, tracing patterns onto her skin.

I don't know what to do with the feelings that are working their way through my body. When I look at Hadley, I feel at peace with the world around me.

I can't remember the last time I was this relaxed.

Hadley yawns and wriggles closer to me. I groan as my cock stiffens at the feeling of her body pressed against mine.

"Well, good morning to you too," Hadley says, her voice raspy with sleep. She looks up at me with those big hazel eyes. The corner of her mouth tips upward as she nestles closer.

"How are you feeling?" I ask, not knowing what else to say to her.

"You're really asking me how I feel?" Hadley's smile grows as her fingers trace the muscles of my stomach. I shudder under her touch, all the blood in my body rushing south.

"I am." I grab her hand and pull it up to kiss her palm. "If you keep touching me like that, then we are never getting out of this bed."

Hadley gives me a wicked smirk and rolls on top of me, straddling my hips. My cock brushes against her core as she swirls her hips. Her nails rake down my chest gently as she looks down at me.

"Maybe I plan on spending all day in this bed with you."

As I look up at her, I don't see any sign of the panic that is currently coursing through my body. If she is freaking out about us waking up together, she doesn't show it.

Despite the mass of emotions that are trying to overwhelm me, I grip her by the hips and pull her up my body until she is hovering over my face.

"If we're going to spend the day in bed, I'm going to need a taste of something sweet first," I say before tracing my tongue along her wet seam.

Hadley moans as I lose myself in her body, throwing my fears to the side for now.

———

THE HOT SPRAY FROM THE SHOWER CASCADES OVER OUR bodies a few hours later as we wash the scent of sex from our skin. Hadley piles her hair on top of her head, holding it with one hand while I lather soap over her body.

"I didn't think that this was the way last night was going to end," Hadley says, tilting her head back to let the spray hit her face.

"Why not?"

I smooth my hands over her ass, taking longer than necessary to massage her flesh. She laughs and steps away from me.

"If that's how long you're going to take to massage my ass, this is going to be a very long shower."

I grin and kneel on the tile behind her, leaning forward and biting her round cheek gently. "Why didn't you think that I was going to want more of that delicious body, Hadley?"

"You don't seem like the kind of man who lingers long," she says, her breath hitching as I bite the other globe.

I settle my hands on her hips and turn her around. Hadley drops her hair, letting it fall down around her. I look at the wet strands plastered across her breasts as I put one hand on her stomach and press her back against the wall.

"You're right about that." I grab one of her thighs and hook it over my shoulder. "But there's something about you that keeps drawing me in."

"Oh yeah?" she asks, breathless as I swipe my tongue along her slit before sucking on her clit.

"Yeah." I nip up one inner thigh and down the other. She moans, her hands sinking into my hair. "I can't decide if it's that smart mouth or your sweet pussy that keeps bringing me back for more."

I swirl my tongue around her clit, teasing her as she writhes against my face. Groaning, I sink my fingers into her, feeling her inner walls clenching around me. Hadley leans back against the wall, angling her hips toward my face.

My cock throbs as I thrust my fingers harder into her.

The water continues to fall around us as Hadley reaches up and starts toying with her nipples. Her moans echo through the tiny shower as I move my tongue in time with my fingers.

"Fuck yes," Hadley says, her pussy starting to pulse as she nears her orgasm.

I groan and slow the pace, not wanting her to finish just yet.

"Do you want to come all over my face like the dirty little slut you are?" I ask, my voice husky as I look up at her.

Heat flashes in Hadley's eyes and her inner walls clench harder around my fingers at the dirty words. I smirk and stop moving, withdrawing from her completely.

"What do you think you're doing?" She tightens her leg over my shoulder.

"You didn't answer my question, Hadley. You want to come, you're going to learn to behave."

"Fat fucking chance of that," she says, her hand leaving her breast to dip between her legs.

I chuckle and swat her hand away before teasing her clit with my tongue again. I drive my fingers into her, feeling her pulse around me. As she nears the edge, I keep teasing her, massaging her inner walls and sucking on her clit.

"Tell me how much you want it," I say as I nip her inner thigh. "Tell me that you want to come all over my face like a dirty little slut and I'll let you do it."

Her leg shakes as my words push her that much closer to the edge. With a mouth like hers, I had been sure she would like a little bit of degradation while I fucked her.

I'm glad to see that I'm right.

"Come on, kitten, tell me how much you want me."

She moans and looks down at me. "Fuck, Jovan. I want to come all over your face like I'm your dirty little slut."

Your dirty little slut.

Giving herself over to me is all it takes to send me into a frenzy. I groan before dipping back between her legs. I flick my tongue over her clit quickly, thrusting my fingers harder and faster.

Hadley's legs start shaking as I twist my fingers and press against the spot I know drives her wild. Her hands drop to the top of my head, her fingers weaving through my hair. She pulls my face closer as her hips rock.

"Come for me," I say before sucking on her clit harder.

Hadley comes hard and fast, slumping back against the wall as her legs shake. Her chest heaves with her rapid breaths as she stares at me.

I lick my lips before getting to my feet. Her nostrils flare slightly as I hold out my fingers to her. "Taste yourself. See how sweet you really are, kitten."

For a moment, I think she is going to tell me to go fuck myself. I can see the words forming on her lips, but instead she takes my fingers in her mouth. She wraps her tongue around my fingers, sucking lightly. Her gaze never leaves mine as she licks my fingers clean before pulling away.

"Kitten?" she asks, an eyebrow arching as she looks at me.

"You fight like a wildcat but I know how to make your pussy purr," I say as I grab the back of her head and pull her to me, my cock throbbing between us. "Kitten seemed fitting."

She closes the distance between us, her mouth sliding against mine. I groan as I tangle my tongue with hers. My hands travel up and down her curves, cupping her breasts and stroking her nipples.

When she hooks a leg around my waist, I slide my hands down to her ass. The water hits my back as I pick her up and press my cock against her core. Hadley wraps her legs around my waist, pulling me closer to her.

"Fuck me," she says as I trail kisses up and down her neck. "Please fuck me. I need your cock."

I chuckle and slide the tip into her before pulling out. "I don't know if you want it bad enough."

"I do. Please fuck me, Jovan."

Her begging sends a shiver down my spine. My cock aches as I slide it along her wet folds. Hadley's fingers sink into my shoulders as I press her back against the wall. She rolls her hips, trying to slide down my length.

I nip her shoulder and thrust into her at the same time. My fingers dig into her hips as I thrust faster. Her inner walls clench around me as I drive myself deeper into her.

"Fuck yes," I say, looking down at where my cock slides into her. "You feel so good wrapped around my cock."

Hadley grazes her teeth along my neck as her legs lock harder around my waist. I thrust harder into her, loving the feeling of her teeth on my body. I groan as she kisses and nips at my neck and collarbones while her pussy squeezes my cock.

I adjust my grip on her, changing the angle. Her clit rubs against me with each thrust. Her moans build as I slam harder into her. I take her wrists in one hand and pin them to the wall above her head.

"I want to feel you milking my cock as you come," I say, rocking my hips faster until her pussy starts pulsing around me. "Come for me, Hadley. Ride me while you come."

She moans, her hands curling into fists as she comes. Her pussy clenches harder around me as my cock aches. I roll my hips as I come, filling her before slumping against her body.

I kiss her shoulder as I pull out of her and take a step

back. I set Hadley down, my arms still wrapped around her waist. She leans against me for a few minutes before stepping under the water.

"You're probably going to have to leave soon," she says, her tone hollow.

Hadley avoids looking at me as I lean against the shower wall and look at her.

"What are you talking about?" I cross my arms, the corner of my mouth pulling up into a smile. "I plan on spending the rest of the day with you."

Her eyes widen as she glances up at me. "Why would you want to do that?"

"Why do you think that I'm just going to walk out of here? Do you think that all I'm after with you is sex?"

She shrugs. "If the shoe fits."

Anger flares within me but I press it down. I don't know how someone like Hadley would think that she has nothing I would want. Nothing that would be worth spending more time with her.

"The shoe doesn't fit, kitten," I say, my voice a low growl. "If you think that this is going to be just a physical thing, then you have another thing coming. I want to know you. And to be quite honest with you, I want to know why Carlos took such an interest in you at the gala."

All the color drains from her face as she lathers the shampoo in her hair. "I don't know what you're talking about."

"Don't play dumb, Hadley. From the looks of things, you and Carlos seemed to know each other well enough. You avoided answering me when we were at the gala."

Hadley presses her lips together in a thin line. "He used to deal everything and anything he could to my parents. He was the first one to talk to me after I found them dead."

I nod, not surprised by what she says. Carlos has always been a snake. Preying on a woman who just lost her parents would be exactly like him.

"What did he want with you?"

I can practically see the walls around her growing taller and stronger as she studies me. There is distrust in her eyes and I know it's from my line of questioning.

To be fair, she has a good reason not to trust me. If I was in her position, I wouldn't trust me either.

"Back then or at the gala?"

"Both."

She shrugs and turns her back to me to rinse the shampoo from her hair. "I don't know what he wanted at the gala."

"And what about back then?"

Hadley sighs, her shoulders slumping. "He wanted to see if there was any money to make. Hold what he could over my head and see where it would get him."

When she looks at me again, her eyes are watery. She shoves the curtain to the side and gets out. I watch as she pulls a fluffy towel around her body, her gaze a million miles away.

I'm going to make sure that he doesn't go anywhere near her again.

Right now, I'm done pressing her for information. If we're going to be spending the whole day together, there is more than enough time to get her to speak.

Although, when I look at her — even though I know she is holding back — I can't bring myself to keep questioning her.

Not when it looks like the answers to those questions could rip her into a thousand tiny pieces.

13

HADLEY

THE MUSIC IS LOUD AND THE DRINKS ARE FLOWING. My feet ache as I hurry back over to the bar. Kennedy smiles at me as she puts a bottle of expensive champagne on her tray.

"How is your night going?" she asks as she grabs several champagne flutes and adds them to the tray. "Because at this point I'm starting to consider quitting and finding somewhere else to work."

I grin and shrug. "It sounds like it's going better than yours. Jovan has a table here tonight and I've got another group as well. Tips should be good tonight. One man already slipped me two hundred dollars for getting the DJ to put on his favorite song."

"Damn," Kennedy says, stepping out of the way so I can grab the bottle of scotch Jovan requested. "I wish that I had your section tonight. The men I'm with keep trying to grab my ass. Rio looks like he might step out of the shadows and start killing people soon."

I put the bottle of scotch on my tray before grabbing some glasses and a little bucket of ice. As I load up the tray,

I look around. Sure enough, Rio is standing in the shadows just behind Jovan's table.

Though he is supposed to be watching his boss, his gaze is firmly on the table Kennedy is working.

"Well, good luck with your drama tonight. If there's a fight, make sure you take a video of it," I say, my tone teasing. "We could probably make some money off that."

Kennedy laughs and shakes her head, her gaze cutting toward Jovan. "How is that whole situation going?"

"He stayed the night the other night," I say, keeping my voice low and making sure that nobody is listening to us. "But you can't go running your mouth about that. I don't want anyone here to know."

Kennedy's eyes nearly bulge out of her head. "You're going to have to give me all the details later. I need to know everything about it."

"You don't need to know anything more than that." I grin and lift my tray, balancing it before stepping out from behind the bar. "The second I give you any details, you're going to tell Rio. The last thing I need is Rio knowing about my sex life."

Kennedy squeals. "Alright, we're going to finish this shift and then you are coming over tonight. I need to know what's going on and I'll give you some of that lemon pie you like so much."

"You made me lemon meringue pie?" My eyebrows raise. "Alright, fine. But you better have some whiskey too."

"I made a pitcher of vanilla whiskey lemonade last night too. You have to try it." Kennedy gives me a smile before turning toward her table. "Meet me outside after work."

"Will do."

Rio glances up at me as I pass him. He looks over my

shoulder and his eyes narrow. Without a word, he moves toward the other table.

Jovan laughs and slaps the shoulder of the man sitting to his right. I ignore whatever it is they're talking about as I put the tray on the ledge that runs behind their table. I fill the glasses with ice before distributing them around the table.

"Hadley, we'd like one of the mixed platters of appetizers for the table," Jovan says as I pour their drinks. "And then another bottle of scotch."

I nod and pour the last glass before setting the bottle back on the ledge with my tray. "Is there anything else I can get anyone right now?"

"Not right now, darling," one of the men says, giving me a smirk. His gaze travels up and down my body. "But maybe once your shift is over there could be something I need help with."

"Enough," Jovan says, his tone sharp as he glares at the man. "Leave her alone, Ricardo. We have business to discuss and I would hate to have to kick you out before we've done that."

Ricardo chuckles and shrugs. "I was just having a little fun with your bottle girl. I'm sure that she would like to have a good time. Working for you must be hell for any sort of social life."

"I'll be back with the platter," I say, hurrying away before Ricardo has the chance to provoke Jovan further.

Though I can still hear them talking behind me, I choose to focus on the music instead. I listen to the pounding beat as I head down the stairs and into the kitchen.

The scent of burger wafts toward me as I go to the machine and enter the order. A ticket pops up and one of the chefs grabs it, calling out the order to everyone else in the kitchen.

Now is as good a time as any to take a break, I think as I take a seat at a little table in the corner.

Pots and pans clang together, accentuated by *fuck this* and *fuck you* every now and then. I grin as I listen to the chaos, enjoying the moment to myself. There is something about sitting in the kitchen and listening to the chefs that makes the stress of my shift fade away.

It's hard to be stressed when there are several people in a competition to come up with the most creative cuss word.

"You know, you're becoming a real problem for me," a woman says as she takes a seat across from me.

"Who are you?" I ask, sitting up a little straighter. "And why am I becoming your problem? I've never even met you."

"Order up!" one of the chefs yells, winking at me as he sets the tray of food in the pass.

I get up and grab the tray, ready to head back out into the club when the girl steps in my way.

"You don't get to just walk around here like you own the place," the woman says. "You think that you're someone because you're Jovan's new girl, but you're not."

"I fail to see what working Jovan's table has to do with anything."

She tosses her inky hair over her shoulder and sniffs. "I'm Erica. I had the best tips in the building until you walked in here. I don't know whose cock you sucked to get such a cushy position, but it ends now. You're fucking with my tips."

I sigh and clutch the platter a little tighter. "Look, if there's a problem with your schedule, you should probably talk to someone about that. Unfortunately, I'm not the person you should be talking to."

"He sleeps with me too," Erica says, a wide grin spreading across her face. "You're nothing special. You think that waiting on his tables is something important but it's just another way to keep you close while he fucks around with everyone here."

I know better than to let her think she's right about what is happening between me and Jovan. "Congratulations? If sleeping with the boss is your thing, then I guess you're a lucky girl. However, I keep my legs closed. Now, if you don't mind, I have to get this tray to my guests."

Even as I brush by her and head out of the kitchen, I'm fuming. Though I know that there is nothing serious between me and Jovan, I'm irritated. I have no right to be jealous, since I keep trying to stay away from him, but I hate knowing that he is sleeping with anyone else.

Especially after what happened between us the other day.

He insisted on spending the day with me. We had a good time. It didn't seem like he was just fucking me to have someone to fuck, but I've been a bad judge of character before.

"Alright, boys," I say a few minutes later as I approach the table. "I have the food and I'll be back with another bottle in a minute."

The men look up and start reaching for food the moment the platter is set in the middle of the table. I step back and turn but a hand wraps around my wrist. Jovan grins up at me, and for a second, I feel like I'm the only person in the room.

"You're doing a great job tonight," he says as he slips a

hundred dollar bill into my hand. "I'm going to talk them into giving you some great tips tonight."

I shake my head and stuff the money in the pocket of my apron. "Don't bother. You'll just put more of a target on my back."

His eyebrows knit together. "What are you talking about?"

"Your little girlfriend with the black hair and the boobs up to her neck thinks that I'm fucking with her tips. Or fucking you. I'm still not sure what the point of her little tirade was."

"Hadley, if there is someone bothering you, I can deal with them."

"Don't bother." I pull my hand away from him. "I can deal with this shit on my own. If you get involved, it's just going to make it worse for me."

"Kitten."

"Nope. Not here. Not anywhere, honestly. I should have known better than to let things get complicated between us."

I walk away from him as the other men start calling his name. His gaze burns into my back as I grab the tray and empty bottle. As I head to the bar, I take a deep breath.

Getting involved in any capacity with Jovan is a bad idea. What happened in the kitchen was just another reminder of that.

———

Hours pass, midnight coming and going before my shift finally ends.

Kennedy yawns as the bright lights come on and the

door downstairs slams. The club is closed for the night and it's time to start cleaning.

"I don't know if I have the energy to come over," I say as I glance at the time on my phone. "It's nearly four in the morning. I have to get some stuff settled for school by lunchtime."

Kennedy hums along with the soft music playing while she kicks off her heels. "You know that you can come over whenever. I just want to get all the details that I can out of you. Who knows when I'll have the chance again."

"I tell you a lot of things," I say as I kick off my own heels and grab a bottle of disinfectant.

She scoffs and tosses me a rag from the pile on the bar. "You do not tell me a lot of things. Hell, the only person I know who is more closed off than you is Jovan."

"I'm going to take that as an insult. I'm not nearly that bad." I spray down two of the tables before wiping them down. "My life just isn't that interesting. There's not much to tell you."

"You have a lot more going on in your life than you're willing to tell me about. That's fine, though. You can keep your secrets. Sooner or later I'll get you drunk and you'll tell me everything."

"Keep holding your breath," I say, feeling a little guilty for not telling her about the baby.

If there is anyone that I'm going to tell about my pregnancy, it will be Kennedy. However, it doesn't feel right to tell her before I tell Jovan. He's the baby's father and he deserves to know.

Maybe.

I still don't want my baby stuck in the cartel life. Nothing good will come of it.

"Come on," Kennedy says, gesturing to the other bottle

service tables. "The sooner we get this cleaned up, the sooner we can leave."

She dances to the beat of the music as we clean. Every now and then, she looks at me like there's something she wants to say. Instead, she keeps her mouth shut and keeps cleaning.

By the time we finish and leave The Brazen, the sun is coming up over the horizon. Kennedy jogs to Rio's car, pausing long enough to wave at me before slipping inside.

"Hey," Jovan says, appearing out of thin air.

I narrow my eyes as my heart races. It's too early in the morning — or late at night — for him to look this good. His gray dress shirt hugs his muscled torso in all the right ways.

"We need to talk about whatever the hell that was in there earlier," he says, crossing his arms as he steps into my path.

"No, we really don't. There's nothing to talk about." I try to step around him but he gets in my way. "Jovan, please."

His expression softens slightly. "Hadley, you know I can help you. Whatever you need."

I shake my head, my heart sinking to my stomach. "You might be able to help me, but at what cost?"

"What are you saying?"

"It was wrong to get involved with you." I brush by him and hurry for my car, pulling my keys out of my pocket. "Please, just give me some space."

Before he can respond, I get in the car and lock the doors. For a minute, I'm not sure whether he is going to step in front of the car so I can't leave or not.

His gaze feels like it's searing me from the inside out. Jovan nods once before stepping to the side. For whatever reason, I can't look away from him.

There is a part of me that thinks I should talk this out. Maybe he would have some insight that I don't.

Maybe he would be able to quiet the green-eyed demon that came out when Erica cornered me.

When it comes down to it, though, I don't know what to say to him.

All I know is that I need to get the hell away from him before my life gets even more fucked up.

Jovan is a beautiful and deadly mistake that I'm determined not to make.

14

JOVAN

"Is she here yet?" I ask Rio as I pace back and forth across the club. "Hadley was supposed to be here ten minutes ago. As soon as Alessio sends me the message with the meeting location, we need to be prepared to go."

Rio nods and pulls out his phone. "She hasn't sent anything to me yet. She's probably just running late. Hadley is reliable. There's no need to worry about her."

Except, there is a reason to worry about her. It's been over a week since she left me standing in a parking lot and wondering what the hell happened.

I sigh and run my hand through my hair. Alessio specifically asked that she be there. I need his help, so she needs to come.

Based on the few times I've talked to Alessio since we set up the meeting, he thinks she's good for me. I'm not sure that I agree, but life would be far more boring without her in it, that's for sure.

And they'll get along great since they have the same sense of humor.

My phone starts ringing and I breathe a sigh of relief when I see Hadley's name flashing across the screen.

"Hadley, where are you?" I ask, my tone a little harsher than intended. "We're waiting for you. Are you close?"

She coughs. "I'm sorry to let you down like this. I've been feeling pretty sick for most of the night and it's only gotten worse this morning. I'm not going to be in today."

I scowl and consider telling her exactly what I think of the fake cough. "Hadley, we have a meeting with Alessio today. A very important one that I need you at. Would you mind coming in for a little bit? Just for the meeting."

I'm gritting my teeth as I try to play nice with her but I'm on the verge of losing my patience.

Alessio is only here today, then he is going back to Atlanta. He was clear that he'll only talk to me about this face-to-face and that he insists on seeing Hadley, so there is no way she is backing out of this. And if I don't get the information I need from Alessio, someone is going to pay.

I don't want that person to be Hadley.

She coughs again, sniffling for added effect. "I'm sorry, Jovan. I really don't think that I'm going to be able to be there. I know how important this meeting is, but I don't think I can make it. I feel really terrible."

"Look, Hadley, if this is just your way of avoiding me, then I need you to put the childish shit to the side and get your ass in here. We have business to take care of and I don't have time to waste playing your games."

"Fuck you," she says, venom in her voice before the call goes dead.

I stare at the phone, anger rolling through me in waves. This isn't how this day is supposed to be going. She isn't even sick. She's trying to avoid me because she's scared of whatever is happening between us.

Hadley is acting like she's the only one who might be freaking out about the other night.

Little does she know, I haven't stopped thinking about it either. Every time I close my eyes, there she is.

"Well, that sounded like it went well." Rio chuckles and busies himself with checking over his gun. "So, we're going to do the meeting without her?"

"Fuck that. Alessio can wait." I pull out my phone and dial Alessio's number, waiting for the rings to end.

"I thought I was supposed to contact you, not the other way around," Alessio says.

"Listen, I need to move the meeting. Hadley says that she isn't feeling well, which means that I need to go over there and figure out why she's lying to me."

"Have you considered that she's telling the truth?" Alessio's tone is sharp. "I have no problem moving the meeting but you need to stop suspecting the worst about people. She doesn't have to be at the meeting either. I was looking forward to spending some time getting to know the woman who was able to bring you to your knees, but if she isn't feeling well, she isn't feeling well."

I roll my eyes. "Look. I'm going over there. How does midnight work for the meeting?"

"It's fine. I'll see you there but do not bring that poor woman if she isn't feeling up to it."

"Yeah. Sure. See you later." I hang up and turn to Rio. "Go get some rest. The meeting will happen at midnight tonight. Be back here for it."

"Alright, boss. Good luck dealing with Hadley."

"I'm not going to need it," I say as I storm out of The Brazen and head for my car.

As I get in, I try to keep the reins tight on my temper. Storming into her apartment and losing my shit is only going to make her less likely to come. I need to approach this with caution.

I know Alessio is okay with her not going, but I'm not. Not if this is her trying to avoid me. I was letting her get her space because I knew she'd be there tonight, so her trying to get out of it is not happening.

However, I need to remember Hadley is acting like a wounded animal who is busy licking her wounds. If I rush her, she will spook.

My hands tighten on the wheel as I head for her apartment.

IT DOESN'T TAKE LONG TO PICK THE LOCK TO HADLEY'S apartment. That's the first sign that something might be wrong with her after all. The deadbolts aren't pulled across and the door opens easily once the lock clicks.

As soon as I step inside, I hear the retching. My stomach turns and guilt immediately starts to claw at me.

Maybe she really is sick. I shouldn't have questioned her on it. Hadley might be secretive, but she has no reason to lie to me.

Actually, she has a lot of reasons to lie to me. Who I am makes it important for her to lie to me about some things. If I were her, I would curate lies to protect myself.

This isn't one of those lies that I would tell, though. I should have believed her when she said she was sick instead of projecting my own issues onto her.

Great, now I sound like a fucking therapist.

I stand a little taller and look around the apartment as I hear the toilet flush. As I head to her bedroom, the bathroom door opens and she appears in front of me with a toothbrush hanging out of her mouth.

"What the hell are you doing here?" she asks, her words distorted. She pulls the toothbrush out of her mouth and glares at me. "Why the hell are you breaking into my apartment?"

"I didn't think you were actually sick," I say, more guilt rising to the surface as her eyes widen slightly. "I thought you were using it as an excuse to avoid me after we spent the other day together."

Hadley rolls her eyes, her nostrils flaring. "You didn't really give me a reason to avoid you. We sat on the couch and watched some movies. There's hardly anything horrifying about that."

"And what about leaving me behind at the club the other night?" I cross my arms, internally berating myself for how childish I sound right now. "How are you feeling?"

She thankfully ignores my first question. "I feel like shit. I haven't stopped throwing up all morning and I'm starving. Except I can't keep anything down either so I've been having a great time."

Dark bags circle her under eyes and her cheeks look hollow. The pale gray tinge to her skin has me rolling up my sleeves and nodding to her bed.

"Get back in bed once you're done with that. I'll make you some soup."

"I don't have soup."

"Brush your teeth and then get back into bed, kitten. I'll figure out everything else."

As I step into her kitchen, I wonder what the cartel would think of me now. Their fearless leader changes his plans for the day to nurse a woman he might care about back to health.

It's not something that they would ever let me live down. That kind of behavior isn't looked too kindly upon in my world. Not from the man who is supposed to be in charge of everyone. Take care of them in a different way.

Making them soup is not that way.

For her, I'm changing. I'm starting to see the human side I thought I killed a long time ago.

I pull open the fridge and start rummaging through the food until I find some vegetables and chicken. Humming to myself, I dump the ingredients on the counter and start looking through the rest of her cupboard for things to cook with.

It doesn't take long to get everything chopped up and in the pot. By the time the broth is boiling, I can hear Hadley's soft snores from the other room.

I leave the food to cook and go sit on her couch. As I sort through the papers on the table, looking for the remote, I see a note in her writing.

Dr. Morris. OBGYN. Prenatal. Nine. Monday.

My heart stops in my chest as I read the words over and over again. I feel like I'm going to be sick as I put the note down before picking it back up again.

Does this mean what I think it means?

I think back on the times that we've had sex and I'm not sure that there's been protection involved in any of them. I can't remember wearing a condom or asking her if she was on any form of birth control.

Rookie fucking mistake, Aguilar. You know better than to fuck around without a rubber.

I groan and run my hands down my face. There is no way that she is pregnant. She would have said something to me if she even thought she was.

At least, I think she would have.

I don't know for sure, though. There are a lot of things I don't know about Hadley. Her reaction to finding out she is pregnant is one of those things.

As I glance toward her room, I consider waking her up and demanding that we get to the bottom of this right now. I want to know if she's pregnant and more importantly, I want to know if the baby is mine.

Neither of us have agreed to be anything with each other. We aren't dating or exclusive in any sense of the word — though there hasn't been anyone else for me since she walked into my life.

I look back down at the note, dragging my hands down my face. I don't know what this means or what I am supposed to do about it.

Since I lost my family, I haven't given much thought to creating a new one. At no point in time did I ever consider having a child with a woman I barely know.

I don't have the time or the mental capacity to think about this right now.

When Hadley wakes up, we can talk about it. I want to believe that she has a good reason for not telling me that she might be pregnant. Maybe she wanted to confirm the pregnancy before she said anything.

After all, she can't be too far along. Unless the baby isn't mine.

Even the thought of her being with another man has me seeing red.

The primal part of me wants to claim her as my own. To whisk her away from where anyone else might interfere with our relationship.

The other part of me is too busy being fascinated with

the ground she walks on too ever consider locking her away. Hadley is a free spirit, meant to live as she pleases.

Outside of the bedroom, there is no controlling her.

I crumple the note in my hand and stuff it in my pocket before going to check on the soup. As I ladle it into a bowl, Hadley walks into the living room. She stretches as she yawns and I'm pleased to see a little more color in her cheeks than there was before.

"Feeling any better?" I ask, my voice tight as I hand her the bowl of soup.

"A bit. Thank you for this," she says as she pulls open a drawer and grabs a spoon. "You really didn't have to. I would have been fine."

"Well, I figured that we had some things to talk about too." I pull the note out of my pocket and put it on the counter between us. "Starting with this. What is this, Hadley?"

"You were going through my things?" she asks, putting the bowl on the counter and glaring at me. "You had no right to do that. Just like you had no right to break into my apartment."

"I hardly broke in. if you can't be bothered to pull the deadbolt across, then you are asking for someone to enter. You're lucky it was me instead of anyone else."

Her eyes widen and her cheeks turn a bright shade of red. "You have got to be fucking kidding me. You don't mean that."

"I do mean that." I scowl and cross my arms. "Now, stop avoiding the question. What the hell is that? Are you pregnant?"

Her gaze flits away from me. "Yes."

"Is the baby mine?"

"As far as I know."

I pace away from her, heading over to the window to look down at the city below. "Now isn't the time for jokes, Hadley. Were you planning on telling me or were you just going to keep this a secret until the baby popped out?"

She shrugs like it doesn't matter. Like what she was going to do with the baby wouldn't matter to me.

It's only the flash of uncertainty that I see in her eyes that lets me know she is as worried about this baby as I am.

"I don't know what I was going to do, okay? You have to admit that with your line of work you aren't exactly the most ideal father."

A pit opens in the bottom of my stomach. "You're right about my job being dangerous. That's why you're packing your shit and moving in with me until the baby is born. I'm not going to have the two of you living in this shit hole and waiting for some criminal to break in."

She gives me a flat look. "That already happened. I don't see how anyone can out-criminal you."

"Funny. Finish your soup and then go pack your shit. You're under my protection now, kitten."

"Look, I'll keep you involved with the pregnancy, but there is no way that I'm going to move in with you. We barely know each other, and to be honest, I don't want to wake up and see your flavor of the week sneaking out every night."

I scoff and shake my head. "Is that really what you think of me? Do you think that there's been anyone else since you walked into my life? Fuck, Hadley, do you think that there could be anyone else?"

"Erica was very clear when she told me about sharing your bed."

"Fucking Erica," I say, my voice barely more than a growl. "I slept with her once, months ago. She's trying to stir shit up for her own entertainment. Is that why you've been avoiding me?"

"One of the reasons," Hadley says. She runs her hand through her hair while looking at me like a deer caught in the headlights. "I know you mean well, but you can't just walk in here and demand that I move in with you. It isn't going to happen."

"It *is* going to happen. You can either move in with me or I will move you in myself."

Hadley's eyes narrow before she spins on her heel and heads for the door. She grabs her keys and slides on her shoes.

"Where do you think you're going?" I ask, my voice booming through the apartment.

"Go to hell, Jovan. You don't get to control me like you control everyone else in your life."

The door slams behind her, leaving me wondering whether or not I should go after her.

Instead, I put the soup in the fridge before heading into her room and packing a bag.

She's going to be staying with me whether she likes it or not. I'm not going to have her risk her life or the baby's.

If Felix finds out about the baby, there is no telling what he will do.

Hadley can hate me all she wants for protecting her.

"I DIDN'T THINK YOU WERE GOING TO MAKE IT BACK IN time for the meeting," Rio says as he gets into my car a few minutes before midnight. "I thought I was going to have to pull off some championship level stalling."

'I'm here now." I tighten my grip on the wheel as I press down hard on the gas, whipping the car around and heading toward the meeting location.

"And snappy. Do you want to talk about whatever is making you grip the wheel like you're trying to kill it?"

"Nope. Have you heard from Hadley about whether or not she is going to be at this meeting?"

Rio shrugs. "I told her where we were meeting. Kennedy told me to pound sand and then I left."

"Fucking women," I say, gritting my teeth together as I pull into the parking lot of a small office building.

Shock runs through me when I see Hadley's car sitting in front of the main doors. She leans against it with her arms crossed and her hair blowing in the slight breeze.

Some of the tension that's been building in my body all afternoon melts away at the sight of her. Other than answering the one message I sent her to make sure she was alright. She hasn't spoken to me.

"Alright, I want you to stay near me," I say as I park the car and get out. "But if things start going sideways in there, then your first and only priority is getting Hadley to safety. While we know that Alessio won't do anything, I can't make any promises about the men he's going to have with him, if we consider what he has going on. And there is also Felix to consider, so stay sharp."

Rio arches an eyebrow, a smug smile on his face. "You say that like I was going to have another plan. I like her a lot more than I like you. Plus, Kennedy would kill me if her best friend died."

"And you want to marry that woman?" I say under my

breath as we get out of the car. "I don't think that I'm ever going to understand you."

"Don't worry about it, boss. One day, you're going to meet a woman who makes you want to be a better man. When that day comes, I'm going to tell that woman to run far and fast."

Rio chuckles as I roll my eyes. He's lucky that he's my friend in situations like these. The man barely has a filter to begin with and he rarely uses it around me. Sometimes I wonder if I should be tougher on him. Hold him to the same standard of respect that everyone else is held to. But life wouldn't be the same without Rio bothering me all the time. He's the one person who manages to keep me grounded and feeling like a person.

I look at Hadley and take in the distant look in her eyes.

Maybe Rio isn't the only person who keeps me grounded.

"Alright, we're going to go in there and, Hadley, don't worry about anything Alessio says. He's a grumpy asshole and he's going to try and get under my skin. He might try to get under yours. It seems like his favorite activity. He's a good man, though."

She gives a sharp nod as Rio stands beside her. Hadley shoots him a small smile before her focus is back on me. "If someone starts shooting, I'm leaving your ass in there."

"I wouldn't expect anything else," I say, trying to hold onto my anger with her instead of the amusement that threatens to take over. "He is my friend and ally, so we should be okay, but if things go sideways, you get out with Rio and I will take care of everything else."

After running over a brief escape plan, we head inside. Our footsteps echo in the stairwell as we climb to the third floor. My heart is racing as I pull open the door and step into the empty lobby.

This is the night where I get the information I've been looking for.

This is the first chance I have at getting rid of the Domingos cartel for good.

I should have killed Felix when I killed the rest of his family.

"Welcome, my friends," Alessio says as he appears from behind a pillar. He stands a good half a foot taller than me and he's built like a brick wall. "Looks like you're feeling better, Hadley."

Hadley nods and smiles at him as Alessio comes over to us and pulls her into a tight hug. She grins as he whispers something in her ear before pulling away. I don't want to know what he said to her. It's only going to bother me.

"Jovan," Alessio says, his gaze shooting toward me. "Just a head's up, we have some other matters to discuss at a later date as well."

His words and the look he gives the men standing just to the side are all it takes to have my guard up. Something isn't right here, especially with the way his gaze drags over Hadley. I can see the concern in his eyes when he looks back at me and stuffs his hands in his pockets.

"What information do you have on our guy?" I ask, crossing my arms and standing a little taller. I glance at the other men, their hands hovering near their guns.

"This is for you." Alessio hands me a folder that was on a nearby desk. "It details everything I know about our friend's building power and gaining support. I was thinking that this could be your Valentine's Day gift from me this year."

"Thank you so much, Alessio. I'll let you get on with your night," I say, my tone stern.

"Before you go, I just wanted to say it was nice finally meeting you, Hadley."

She smiles at him and says, "Likewise. And thank you for having my back that first day back at the club. It meant a lot to me."

He looks into her eyes before saying, "No problem. Everyone deserves a second chance when they are trying to get their feet under them the right way."

Her cheeks go a light shade of pink. "Thank you."

"I liked your fire that first day, and from everything Jovan has told me about you, you seems like a good woman, so I have a favor to ask."

I step closer to Alessio, ready to intervene if he says something that upsets Hadley.

"What is it?" she asks, curiosity burning in her eyes.

"Never stop giving him hell, huh?"

Hadley laughs. A beautiful sound that I'd never heard from her before. So genuine. So heartfelt.

"I promise," she says when she calms down.

"Now, let me talk to this guy in private for a second, okay? It really was a pleasure meeting you."

"Likewise. Please come visit more often. I had fun." She heads up out and Rio follows.

When they are out of earshot, Alessio shakes his head. "Someone is after your girl. I heard a rumor her parents are still alive. I'm not sure how accurate that is, but I thought I'd let you know in case you wanted to look into it."

"The fuck?"

"I'm sorry I couldn't bring any good news this time, but you can count on my support if you need it."

"Thank you, man. I really appreciate it."

He nods and follows the path Rio took to the stairwell, his men trailing behind him, leaving me alone with the folder.

Can Alessio's intel be right about Hadley's parents? And if it is, is she involved in their ruse in any way?

My mind is going a thousand miles an hour.

One way or another, I'm going to get to the bottom of whatever the fuck is going on in my city.

15

HADLEY

I take a deep breath as I stand outside Jovan's office door, still trying to get a hold of myself. After I left last night, I went home only to find some of my things gone. If he thinks that he can force me to move in with him, he's messing with the wrong woman.

As soon as I'm sure I can talk to him without imploding, I knock on his door. There is no sound on the other side, so I open the door a crack and peer in.

Jovan is shrouded in darkness, the only light in the room coming from the small slit between the curtains and a dim lamp in the corner.

"What is this?" I ask as I step inside and close the door behind me. "Some sort of brooding cave?"

"Something like that."

"Why did you want to see me?" I ask, keeping my tone light and professional as I take a seat in one of the chairs on the opposite side of the desk.

He looks up at me and shrugs. "I thought that there were some things you and I should talk about. Yet again, you ran away before I had the chance. I know you were a damaged child, but running away at every turn isn't going to benefit you."

I grip the arms of the chair, trying to keep my temper in check. "Unfortunately, I had somewhere else I needed to be. Kennedy was expecting me and I couldn't keep her waiting. Besides, I quit, so it's not like you are my boss anymore."

Jovan steeples his fingers together beneath his chin. The expression on his face makes it clear that he doesn't believe my lie.

Even though I think I can trust him with the truth, there is something that keeps holding me back. If there is anyone who isn't going to judge me for my past, I know it's Jovan.

The scared little girl in me doesn't think that, though. She thinks that it is better to keep my secrets to myself for now. She doesn't want me to spill everything to him in case he turns his back on me like everyone else in my life has done.

I just want to hold onto this one good thing for a little longer.

"Kennedy would have waited for you for hours. And I don't accept your resignation. Now that that's settled, what else are you hiding from me, Hadley?"

"So, it's Hadley when you're pissed at me and kitten when you want to fuck me senseless?"

He chuckles darkly and leans forward, resting his arms on the desk. "I'm not in the mood to play games with you, *kitten*, even if it is one of my favorite pastimes."

"What can I help you with?"

"I want to know more about your parents."

"Why? My parents are dead. I saw their bodies."

"And you have no reason to believe that they could still be alive?"

I'm speechless. "What? No!"

"Okay, how did you find out? Did someone come to your school and tell you?"

"I found them. They were lying on the floor when I got home from work after school one day. I tried to get them to wake up, but they wouldn't. They weren't breathing, so I called Carlos and he called nine-one-one. They were declared dead on site."

I was free. A bittersweet feeling. No more abuse, on one hand. On the other, I could now only count on myself, since I was all alone in the world. So, a few days later, in a fit of anger after a particularly nasty nightmare, that was more of a memory, I set fire to the house to make sure there were no reminders of them. Maybe like the phoenix, I could rise from the ashes of my childhood home.

Though I know I should tell him that, I can't say the words. I'm terrified that he's going to hear what I've done and think that I'm a monster.

Who tries to burn their dead parents' house down to try to hide away years of abuse? Or maybe I was trying to burn the abuse itself away. No luck there, though.

"Alright, so they're dead and Alessio was given bad intel."

Alessio was told my parents were alive?"

"Yes, but why would someone do that? Why would someone spread the word that your parents are not dead?"

"I don't know. I have no clue who Alessio is or why he would care about my parents. You have to believe me."

The room starts to feel warmer and smaller as he studies me. His eyes narrow and he gets up, stepping around the desk to stand in front of me. Jovan's soft hair falls in his eyes and I picture running my fingers through that hair to get it out of his face.

I remember how soft his hair was in my hands as I held

him while he gave me the best orgasm I've had in a long time. The tender looks he gave me when he made me beg for his cock.

That isn't the man standing in front of me anymore. Not by a long shot.

The man in front of me is the leader of a cartel and a person who may see fit to dispose of me at any moment. He is the kind of man who could get rid of me without a second thought.

"Hadley, why the hell should I believe anything that is coming out of that pretty little mouth of yours when all you do is lie to me?" he asks, his voice low and dangerous as he leans closer to me.

"I've never lied to you."

He smirks, trailing a finger along the curve of my cheek. "No, that's right. You don't lie to me. You just keep secrets from me and run away. You hide even though we both know you have a backbone. What I can't figure out is what you're hiding, though."

"You have your secrets. I have mine."

Jovan sits up straight. "My baby is not a fucking secret, Hadley."

"And we're back to the baby!" I stand up and shake my head. "I was going to tell you about the baby after I had more time to process what I wanted to do. Life with you isn't the kind of life that a child should have. Can you honestly tell me without a doubt that you can keep our child safe?"

"How could I tell you that when you haven't even given me a chance to plan for it?" He jerks his chin in the direction of the chair. "Sit your ass back down. We're not done talking yet."

"I think I'm done talking."

I head for the door, my hand closing around the handle just as I feel a hand on my waist. I'm spun around quickly and pinned against the wall. Jovan looks down at me, irritation crossing his handsome features. There are only mere inches between us.

Excitement courses through my body as he grinds his stiffened cock against me. In that moment, the argument fades away. There is nothing but the sexual chemistry between us.

When Jovan is rough and demanding like this, I reach a new level of turned on. I want him to take what he wants from me and leave me a writhing mess at the end of it all.

That's probably what scares me the most.

"Listen and listen good, kitten. We need to talk about this baby and figure out a plan. I was wrong to take your things last night, but I am not going to allow you to put both yourself and the child in danger because you won't let go of your pride."

"My pride?" I scoff and try to wriggle away from him but he only presses his body against mine harder. "Let me go. If I'm not out of a job, I'm supposed to be working right now and everyone is going to wonder where I am."

He chuckles and leans forward to take my earlobe between his teeth. "We could let them all hear where you are. I could fuck you up against this door and everyone out there would hear the moans you make when you come."

I would be lying if I said he didn't incinerate my underwear with his words.

"Now," he says as he pulls back from me. "I want to take you for a weekend away so we can discuss all of this properly without any outside distractions. I have a nice cottage in the woods upstate. There's a small town close by. I would like to take you there."

"And all we're going to do is talk?" I ask, suspicion crawling through me.

He gives me a wolfish grin. "We could do other things if you'd like."

I reach out and run my hand slowly over the tented material of his pants. "You would like that, wouldn't you?"

"Stop being a tease, kitten. You're going to go back to work and pretend as if nothing has happened in here. Once you're done with your shift, I'm taking you away from here so we can figure out our shit together."

"Alright," I say, knowing that there is no avoiding this.

It's time that I talk to Jovan, at least a little bit. He is the father of my baby and I haven't been fair to him. I owe him some explanations — though there are secrets I plan on keeping to myself.

While I may allow him to see more glimpses of my life, the full story is more than anyone else should have to bear.

AFTER SIX HOURS IN THE CAR WITH JOVAN, I'M READY to get out and walk around. While the drive to the cottage has been nice, I'm not a fan of being trapped in a car for a long period of time.

"Jovan turns off the main road and onto a dirt one. Trees line either side of the road and the scent of wildflowers enters the car on the breeze. The sun is shining overhead, even though it is still early in the morning.

"Do you want to go for a nap?" Jovan asks as a large stone and glass house appears in front of us. "I know you worked a long shift and you haven't slept in the car at all."

"Maybe," I say, leaning forward in my seat to get a

better look at the towering house. "This is what you're calling a cottage?"

"Yes." He grins and reaches over to put his hand on my knee. Based on the way his thumb is absentmindedly stroking my bare skin, I'm not sure that he knows he's even doing it.

That simple touch is enough to make butterflies erupt in my stomach. It's the kind of casual touch that speaks volumes. Even when he isn't paying attention to what he's doing, he's reaching for me.

Panic rises along with the butterflies as my mind spirals about what this could mean.

Calm down, Hadley. You're here to talk about what all of this means and where the two of you are going to go from here. Get out of your own head and just start talking to him.

"It's a gorgeous house," I say as he parks the car. "Did you buy it or did you build it?"

"A little bit of both." He points to a wooden part of the house. "That part was built by my grandfather when he and my grandmother first retired out here. He said that he always wanted to build his own little log cabin."

"So, you got it and you added to it?"

Jovan nods and gets out of the car. I reach for my door handle but he is already there and opening the door before I get my seatbelt off.

"Thank you." I put my hand in his and allow him to help me out of the car.

If we are going to spend the next few days up here, I may as well try to go along with his plans. I don't want us to have a horrible relationship if we are going to be bringing a baby into this world together.

I want our child to have the best example of co-parents that they can.

You could be more than just co-parents if you allow your-self to open up to him and go after what you want.

I decide to let the chips fall where they may this week-end. I'm going to let everything play out before me instead of getting wrapped up in my own mind about the *what ifs* and the *maybes*.

I owe it to us to give this thing a chance.

"If you have a gorgeous place like this, why bother living in Miami at all?"

Jovan shrugs and gets our bags from the trunk. "My business is in Miami. Running it from out here isn't possi-ble. Even if it was, I wouldn't want that shit to bleed into this part of my life. This little cottage is the only thing I have left of my family."

My heart aches as his voice sounds a little choked up. "I'm sorry to hear that."

He looks at me and arches an eyebrow. "Do you really not know what happened with my family or are you playing a game with me?"

I grab one of the bags from him and sling it over my shoulder. No sooner do I have the weight comfortable settled on my body than Jovan takes the bag back and starts heading for the house.

"I make it my mission to stay as far away from the cartel and their business as possible."

"Why do you have such an aversion to the cartel? As far as I know, you have no true connections, other than Carlos. And he is just a high level dealer. Nobody of any standing."

I wait while he opens the front door, trying to come up with the right words to describe the way I feel about the cartel without giving away too much.

"The cartel touches everything in Miami and it taints it. I wanted to keep my life as untainted as possible. My parents put me through enough hell when I was younger and I was determined to avoid all of it as I got older."

"You know, I sense a story there that I'm dying to hear."

"Maybe later," I say, yawning through the last word. "I could really use a nap, though .I should have slept on the drive up here but I have a hard time sleeping in cars these days."

He looks at me with curiosity shining in his eyes before leading me through the house. I look around at the wood floors and the massive windows with the view of the outdoors. Everything around me looks like it came from a magazine about a sleek and modern farmhouse.

"Why do you have trouble sleeping in cars?" he asks as he opens the door at the end of the hall to reveal a large bedroom. "I don't have any of the other bedrooms renovated yet, so I hope you don't mind sharing a bed."

"I'm pregnant with your baby. I think that sharing a bed with you is the least of my worries." I give him a cheeky smile as I shimmy my denim shorts down my legs. "Besides, right now. I'm too tired to care."

"Are you going to answer my question?" he asks as he sets the bags on a chair in the corner before stripping down too. "Or is this going to be another one of those mysteries that I'm still trying to unravel about you?"

"I used to live in my car. After my parents died. The house was burned. I had to live somewhere but there was no way in hell I was going to allow myself to get involved with the foster system. So, car it was."

He looks at me for a moment before wrapping his arms around my waist and hauling me against his body.

For a second, I stand there stiffly, not quite sure what's happening. He chuckles and drops a kiss to my shoulder.

"I'm hugging you, Hadley. It wouldn't hurt you to hug me back."

I laugh and wrap my arms around him. The feeling of just standing there and holding onto him is foreign. I can't remember the last time that someone just held me while I stood there with them.

"Come on," he says when he finally steps away. "Nap time."

Jovan gets into bed before pulling the sheets to the side. He holds them open long enough for me to finish kicking off my shoes and shorts. I climb into the bed beside him, careful to keep a good amount of distance between us.

He rolls onto his side and tucks an arm under his head. An amused smile curves his mouth upward. "What are you doing all the way over there?"

"Going to sleep. It's what you should do too."

He shuffles closer to me and wraps an arm around my waist. As his fingers trail up and down my skin, a shiver races down my spine.

Jovan's gaze drops down to my mouth, sending a rush of heat straight to my core. My breath hitches as he leans closer to me.

"You know that I'm going to do whatever I can to keep you and the baby safe, right? I lost my family once. I'm not going to let that happen again."

I want to argue with him about being his family, but I know it's only because of my own fucked up issues. We've both been alone for so long that I don't know if either of us really knows what a family is.

"I'm scared about what's going to happen. I didn't think that I would be having a baby at this point in my life. I'm supposed to finish school and start teaching."

"Who says you can't do that with a baby?" Jovan asks, his tone soft as he continues to trace patterns on my skin.

"I don't have any support. You're running a cartel. I don't have siblings. I'm sure Kennedy would love to help, but I can't rely on her to take care of the baby all the time."

"We have time to figure all that out. I'm not going to leave you to do this on your own."

A lump in my throat threatens to choke me as I look at him. My heart pounds in my chest as I close the distance between us, drifting my lips across his.

Jovan lets out a low groan, his hand flattening against my back as he pulls me too him. The kiss deepens, his tongue tangling with mine. I moan into the kiss as my hand slides over his cheek, feeling the rough stubble against my palm. My hand slides down to his neck as my fingers sink into the soft hair at his nape.

His rough hands slide beneath my shirt before pulling it off me. He grabs my hips and rolls over, pulling me on top of him. His cock throbs against my core as I roll my hips and tease him.

"Fuck, Hadley," he says, his voice raspy as he pulls back to look at me. "I don't know how I've gone this long in my life without you."

I don't know what to say to that, so I kiss him again. I smooth my hands over his bare chest as I pepper kisses along his cheek and down his neck to his collarbones. I graze my teeth along the sensitive skin before continuing to work my way down his body.

Jovan lifts his hips enough for me to pull off his shorts and boxers. His cock springs free, a drop of moisture glistening on the head. I lick the drop from the tip of his cock before dragging my tongue along his length.

I grip the base of his cock while I take the head in my mouth. Jovan's fingers sink into my hair and he pulls it back from my face. Our gazes connect as I swirl my tongue around him. He groans, heat blazing in his eyes, as I hollow my cheeks and take more of him into my mouth.

I tease him with my teeth and tongue, sucking his cock and moaning when he hits the back of my throat. I moan around him as he guides my head faster, his hips raising up as he thrusts deeper into my mouth.

"I need to feel your pussy wrapped around my cock," he says, his voice gruff as he pulls me away from his cock.

As I work my way back up his body, he unclasps my bra and tosses it to the side. I trace his abs with my tongue before sitting up and straddling his hips.

"Hope you're not too attached to that thong," he says before he grips the lace and rips it away from my body.

Heat pools between my legs as I hover over his cock. Jovan's fingers find my clit, swirling around the sensitive bud as he stares up at me. I lean forward and trace my tongue over the inky black lines on his shoulders that stem from the crying angel tattoo on his back.

"If you keep that up, I'm not going to last long," he says, his voice a little more than a growl as his hand sinks into my hair.

He pulls my head back and forces me to look at him before driving his cock upward and sinking into my pussy. I moan as I place my hands on his chest and start to rock my hips, taking him deeper and deeper. I take his cock to the hilt, my pussy pulsing around his throbbing cock.

"Eyes on me, kitten. I want to see your face when you come all over my cock."

"Fuck." I dig my nails into his chest as he pulls my hair

harder. "Yes. Fuck. I need more. Please. I want to come all over your cock."

Jovan smirks up at me before pulling out. "Get on all fours."

I don't hesitate to do as he says. My body is aching for him and I'm on the edge of an orgasm. I need more, and at this moment, I'm willing to do whatever he says to get it.

"What a good little slut," he says, his fingers trailing down my spine and over the curve of my ass.

His fingers slide through my wet folds before dipping inside me. My inner walls clench around him as my hips rock into him.

I need more.

"Please," I say, my voice breathy as he curls his fingers and rocks them deeper into me.

"What do you want, Hadley?"

"I want to come."

"I don't know if you've been good enough to deserve that," he says, his voice husky as he presses a hand into the middle of my back and pushes me down on the bed. The sheets are silky against my breasts, the friction between my body and the fabric making my nipples harder.

Jovan replaces his fingers with his cock, his hands gripping my hips and dragging me back against him. I fist the sheets as I arch my back and lift my ass higher, changing the angle until he is buried deep in me.

His hand comes down on my ass, leaving a sharp sting as he thrusts harder and faster. His cock is throbbing inside me as I come, my body shaking. Jovan chuckles and tightens his grip, pulling me back harder against his body with each rock of his hips.

"Fuck, your pussy is squeezing the life out of me." Jovan

groans as he moves faster, slamming into me until he comes. He stiffens for a moment before he slides out of me.

When he falls to the bed beside me and pulls me into his arms, I start to wonder if every night could be like this.

It's a dangerous thought but it's one that I can't shake even as I fall asleep.

16

JOVAN

I LOOK OVER AT HADLEY AS WE WALK AROUND THE TINY town near my cabin. She is smiling and snapping dozens of pictures with her phone. The town looks nothing like Miami, so I understand her fascination. There's something about the little town that has always felt magical to me.

The buildings are all short and painted bright colors. Flowers grow along the storefronts. Grass and trees separate the sidewalk from the road. There are a few cars that drive along, but most people walk.

"I didn't even know there was a place like this anywhere near home," Hadley says as she turns to me and raises her phone to take a picture. "Smile. I want something to remember this day with."

"The other pictures you've taken aren't good enough?" I tuck my hands in my pockets and smile at her, waiting until the phone lowers before shaking my head. "I don't know why you would want a picture of me."

She shrugs and slips her phone into her back pocket. "Our baby is going to want to know what their dad looked like when we met."

The mention of the baby makes my stomach twist and turn. I know that Hadley is hesitant about connecting herself closer to my cartel, but it is the best way to protect the baby. My people would never let anything happen to my child.

One way or another, I'm going to have to make her see that I'm right about this.

Especially when someone seems to have it out for her by spreading lies about her parents. I triple checked the story she told me and she's right. Her parents are dead and buried. So, she has no one else to protect her.

"Have you thought more about moving in with me until the baby is here?"

Though I phrase it as if she will be free to leave once the baby is born, she won't be. I lost my family once. I'm not going to lose my new one. If she wants to move out of my house after the baby is born, I'll build her a house of her own on my property.

No matter what, I'm not going to be letting either of them out of my sight.

Hadley sighs and pulls her hair over one shoulder, toying with the soft curls. "Jovan, I really think it's a bad idea. I want to keep our baby away from the cartel. Living with you and watching the shit that goes on in that life isn't something I want for the baby."

"And what about what I want for the baby?"

She stops and faces me, a million different emotions flashing across her face. "I don't know what to tell you. Your life is dangerous. There no way to make sure that the baby is away from all the shit that follows you if we're living in the same house."

I cross my arms and step closer to her, keeping my voice low. Even though the town is quiet and I'm friends with several people here, I keep my business to myself. There is no reason to bring anything that has to do with the cartel up here.

"Haven't you figured out that people will realize I have a child? I'm sure as fuck not staying away from my child. Sooner or later someone will make the connection either way. If you're with me, it's easier to protect both of you."

She bites her bottom lip and shakes her head. "Can we just have a nice day together instead of arguing about this? When we get back to Miami, we can talk about it."

I scowl but back down. Whether she knows it or not, she won't have a choice in the matter once we get back to the city. Making her move in with me is going to piss her off, but I'm beyond caring about that right now.

Their safety comes first.

Maybe there is a way to make this work without forcibly removing her from her life. I don't want her to hate me. I don't want to control her.

I just want her safe.

"Alright, we don't have to go into detail right now. However, before we talk about this again, will you at least consider allowing me to assign a couple men to protect you?"

"You want me to think about bodyguards?" Hadley looks like an argument is on the tip of her tongue as she puts her hands on her hips. After a moment, her shoulders drop and she nods. "Fine, I'll think about that."

"Thank you," I say as I take her hand and pull her to me.

The frown melts off her face and a smile takes over as I loop my arms around her waist. She runs her fingers through my hair, pushing it back from my face.

"You know, there's a place around here that has an

amazing bacon cheeseburger." I kiss her quickly and hold her a little tighter. "I was thinking cheeseburgers and a milk-shake sound like a pretty good idea."

She raises an eyebrow, a smile curving the corner of her mouth. "The leader of a cartel wants to get burgers and share a milkshake?"

I chuckle and run my hands along the curves of her waist and hips. "Don't go telling people when we get back to the city. It will ruin all the credibility I have."

Hadley kisses me, her mouth slanting against mine in a kiss that is slow and sweet. It's the kind of kiss that makes me think of a future where I get to spend the rest of my life with my new family.

"Well, lucky for you, I can keep a secret." She steps out of my embrace and takes my hand. "Lead the way to the burgers. Me and the baby could use something to eat."

I weave my fingers through hers and head down the street to the diner. "Maybe if you're nice, I'll even buy you one of their famous chocolate pie slices for dessert."

Hadley laughs, and the sound is music to my ears. Seeing her happy is worth the rough moments that we've had together.

I could easily spend the rest of my life living to hear that laugh.

It's after midnight when we fall into bed that night. While Hadley falls asleep easily, I sit in the chair by the window and read a book. The light is dim but she doesn't seem to even notice that it's on as she rolls over and buries her face in the pillows. I smile as I watch her, wondering how I'm going to go back to a life without her falling asleep in my bed every night.

I can't let that happen.

My phone buzzes in my lap as I turn the page in my book. With a sigh, I set the book on the table and turn off the light. The phone keeps ringing as I slip out of the bedroom and close the door behind me.

"Hello," I say as I enter the kitchen and turn on the lights that run beneath the cabinets.

"Hey, boss," Rio says. He sighs and I can hear shuffling in the background. "We have a problem."

"What kind of problem? Do I need to get Hadley out of here? Has Felix found out about her?"

Rio mutters a curse under his breath as something thuds in the background. "Sorry, boss. Kennedy decided that she was going to move all the furniture in the apartment. Apparently, I need to walk into the coffee table at two in the fucking morning."

"Move it all back later. What's the problem?"

"I went to check on Hadley's apartment like you asked. Felix has been there."

The world around me comes to a screeching halt. The game that Hadley and I have been playing — pretending that we're just a couple on vacation — had to come to an end sooner or later.

Felix Domingos is a man with a mission and he isn't going to rest until he's destroyed everything I have left.

It's what I would do if I were him.

It's what I already did.

"How do you know that it was Felix?" I ask as I lean against the counter.

"He left a note. Said that he would be coming for her

sooner than you think. There wasn't much else on the note, other than a promise to kill her."

The blood drains from my body and my head begins to spin. I used to pride myself on being calm under pressure but when it comes to Hadley, I can't seem to think straight at all.

"I want people assigned to watch that apartment every single fucking day. I don't want anyone near her home that we don't know." I push off the counter and head outside, needing the cold night air to clear my head a little.

As I stand on the back deck, the fear of what can happen to Hadley and our baby threatens to consume me. I have to do everything that I can to keep her safe.

"After you have people ready and watching over her home, start getting together everything we need to move her out. We have to move quickly and not give her time to think about it. If she knows that it's coming, she'll make the entire process hell."

"Do you really think that it's a good idea to force her into that?"

I lean against the railing and look out over the backyard. "I know that it's not a good idea, but there is no other way if he knows where she lives. I want her to have a few days after we get back to settle in. After that, we have to move her. I'll make sure she has a day off scheduled and that's the day we'll do it. She'll see that she has no choice in the matter."

"Yes, boss," Rio says, disapproval clear in his voice. "It's your funeral."

"Leave worrying about what Hadley is going to do to me. Just get ready to move her entire apartment in a couple days."

"Alright."

Rio ends the call before I can talk to him about anything else. While I know that he doesn't approve of the plan, it's the only one I can see right now.

Felix is already breaking into her apartment. A few of my people stationed outside at all hours of the day aren't going to stop him if he wants to get her.

She's safer with me than she is with anyone else.

I can protect her.

I won't let her die like my family did.

Hadley is going to move in with me and she's going to be safe. I'm not going to let Felix get to her or our baby. I need her where I can control the environment.

I'm not going to fail her like I've failed so many other people. Hadley is going to be safe with me whether she likes it or not. Sooner or later, she will see that this is for her own good.

While I can understand she doesn't want the baby to be raised in the cartel, the fact remains that the baby is my heir.

She could run with the baby to the other side of the world and Felix would find her.

My other enemies would find her.

I take a deep breath and tuck my phone into my pocket. While I should stay out here longer to clear my head, all I want to do is crawl into bed beside Hadley and go to sleep. I want to feel her safe in my arms and know that everything is going to be alright.

After I head inside, I make sure that all the windows and doors are locked. As soon as I'm sure that we're locked up, I slip back into the bedroom.

To my surprise, Hadley is sitting up in bed with the lamp on. She puts her phone to the side and smiles at me, though she looks like she's barely awake.

"Everything alright?" she asks, her eyebrows knitting together as I put my phone on the dresser.

"It's fine. I just had to take a call."

"Do we need to go back early?" She seems a little more alert as she leans back into the pillows. "I can get packed and be ready to be out of here in an hour if we need to."

I chuckle and shake my head, kneeling on the foot of the bed. "So eager to get away from me."

Hadley's concerned expression waves slightly. "Are you sure that nothing is going on? You would tell me, wouldn't you?"

"Nothing is going on." I grab her ankles and pull her toward me across the bed.

Hadley laughs as I hook my fingers in her shorts and pull them down her long legs. "And what do you think you're doing?"

"You look like you could use a little relaxing. Might help you go back to sleep."

"You promise that nothing is wrong?" she asks, her voice breathy as I nip and suck my way up one leg and down the other.

"I promise nothing is wrong." I suck on the sensitive flesh of her inner thigh as her fingers sink into my hair. "Now, let me play with this pretty pussy until you are too tired to keep worrying about me."

She laughs but it's abruptly cut off when I slide my tongue along her wet slit. My fingers follow the path of my tongue, swirling around her clit as I nip at her pelvic bones.

Hadley moans as I kiss my way back down to her clit. As I circle the little bundle of nerves with my tongue, I thrust my fingers into her.

"Fuck," I say, groaning as my cock stiffens. "You're always so wet for me."

Hadley gasps as I curl my fingers, pressing them against the spot I know drives her wild. Her hips buck as I hook an arm around her thigh to hold her in place.

Her back arches off the bed as I thrust my fingers harder into her, my tongue flattening against her clit. Hadley pulls at my hair as I push her closer and closer to the edge.

I suck on her clit before nipping at her inner thigh. She writhes beneath me as I trace a pattern on her skin with my tongue. I suck on the sensitive flesh until there is a dark mark looking back at me.

"Did you just mark me?" she asks, amusement in her voice as I rock my fingers faster, massaging her inner walls.

"You're mine, Hadley. There's no fucking question about that."

All it takes is another deep thrust as I suck on her clit to have her coming. Her wetness coats my hand as I slow my pace, teasing her and dragging out the orgasm until her body is shaking.

"That's one," I say as I prop myself up on an elbow to look at her. "You're going to keep count of the rest for me like the good little slut that you are."

When her pussy pulsates around me, I know I'm a goner.

I meant it when I told her that she is mine.

17

HADLEY

"You have to tell me all about your trip," Kennedy says as she flops onto my couch with a plate of pizza in her hands. "I can't believe that Jovan took you to a cabin in a tiny town. That's not like him."

I shrug and put a few slices of pizza on my plate. "It was good. It's nice to be back, though. I can't wait to get back to work. I've finally got enough money to pay for school and almost enough to cover my expenses for the year."

"You can't tell me that the highlight of your trip was waiting to get back to work." Kennedy laughs and shakes her head. "No. There has to be more to it than that. I want all the dirty details."

My cheeks warm as I sink into the couch beside her and shake my head. "There aren't that many details. It was some incredible sex. He was great to be around and I had a wonderful time. We only argued once about my living situation."

Kennedy hums and looks away from me, suddenly interested in everything but our conversation. There is a guilty look on her face that instantly has me suspicious.

"Kennedy, what is going on?" I ask, putting my plate on the coffee table and turning to face her. "You look like you have a secret."

She frowns and turns to face me. Kennedy crosses her legs and stuffs a slice of pizza in her mouth, trying to stall. I cross my arms and wait for her to finish eating.

"Men are idiots. I'm not supposed to tell you what's going on because I wasn't supposed to hear it in the first place. I've been arguing with Rio about it for the last couple days."

"Arguing with Rio about what?"

My stomach lurches as car doors slam outside. When I get up and go to the window, Rio and Jovan are walking toward the building. They're carrying stacks of empty boxes while other men trail behind them.

"What the hell is this?" I ask, my tone sharp as I turn to face Kennedy. "You knew about this and you're on their side?"

"I'm not on their side, I'm just in a difficult position. If you want to sneak out, I can stall them. You know that sooner or later he'll track you down, though. Jovan is a powerful man."

I sigh and run my hand through my hair. Though I know what a difficult position Kennedy is in, I can't help but feel a bit betrayed. She should have told me as soon as she found out what Jovan was planning.

Instead, she left me to be blindsided by this mess.

"You're right. I'm not going to take off. He'll just track me down and drag me back. However, if he thinks that he is going to be able to get away with this shit without a fight, he has another thing coming."

I grab my pizza and put it in the kitchen before going to

wait by the door. As soon as there is a knock I pull it open and stand in Jovan's path.

"What the fuck do you think you're doing?" I ask, my tone bright and cheerful even though I'm fuming inside.

How dare he think that he can march in here and order me to move in with him. Especially after the talk we had.

When we got back from his cabin, we talked about allowing people to watch over me. I've had men following me around everywhere I go, making sure that I'm safe. I thought it was enough of a compromise to get Jovan to take a step back. I didn't think that it was only a temporary situation before he stormed in here.

"There's been a change in plans. You're going to be moving in after all." His gaze meets mine with a look that leaves little room for argument.

At least, that's likely what he thinks.

"I told you that I was fine with people watching over me. What's changed from the other day to now?"

"Nothing," he says through gritted teeth. "Just let me in so we can get your shit packed. You're moving tonight."

"Like hell I am. We might have something going on, but that doesn't mean you get to control my life."

I step back and let him and the others in, but only because I don't want my nosey neighbors to hear the conversation. After I close the door behind them, I turn to Jovan, ready to keep arguing about my freedom.

"Hadley, please don't argue with me. I just want to make sure that you and the baby are safe." He tosses the stack of boxes onto the counter. "And to be honest, I don't care how that makes you feel right now. Your safety is my first priority. If that means that I have to kidnap you, then that's what I'm going to do."

Kennedy steps between us and looks up at Jovan. "This is wrong, please don't do this."

"Stay out of it," Rio says as he hooks Kennedy around the waist and pulls her out of the way. "Come help me pack her clothing before one of the others gets to it. You know they'll be itching for the chance to go through a woman's underwear drawer."

I sigh and look over at Kennedy. While I appreciate her trying to help, I don't want her to put herself in a position that's only going to cause problems in her life.

"It's fine, Kennedy," I say with a tight smile. "Go with Rio. I can handle this myself."

Jovan watches me as Kennedy and Rio head into my bedroom. The other men busy themselves with packing up the kitchen and living room. Their ability to ignore the tension in the room is amazing.

"If nothing has changed, then why has our agreement changed?" I take a step toward him, tilting my head slightly to look him in the eyes. "Jovan, what the hell is going on? If there's a threat to our child, then I need to know."

"We'll discuss everything later. Right now, I need you to get packed. One way or another, you're going to be moving."

I don't know why I stop arguing with him in that moment. Maybe it's the tone of his voice or the despair in his eyes. Something is going on if he is going back on his agreement.

For as long as I have known him, Jovan has always been a man of his word.

If he's stepping in now, he has to have a reason.

Though it is a giant leap of faith, I choose to trust him.

Please don't let this be a mistake.

"Are you ready to tell me why I'm living with you now?" I ask, my tone sharper than intended as Jovan carries the last of my boxes into his house.

"Hadley, can't you just trust that I am doing what is best for you? I don't see why I need to explain myself to you every step of the way. Believe it or not, there are some things that you're better off not knowing."

I scowl at him, trying to keep a lid on my temper. Whatever is happening scares him. I've seen the long glances he gives me when he thinks I'm not looking. The way his eyes track me around the room, making sure that I'm never out of his sight for long.

"We're partners in some sense of the word," I say, sitting on the counter. Jovan sighs and starts pulling food out of the fridge and dropping it on the counter. "We're going to have a child together. I need to know who or what is a threat to our baby beyond your job."

"What makes you think that it would be anything outside of cartel business?" He doesn't look at me as he pulls out a knife and a cutting board.

Jovan rolls up his sleeves and starts chopping the vegetables as I consider walking out. I know that he hasn't made a habit of answering to anyone else in his life, but that's going to have to change now.

I'm not going to unknowingly put our baby in danger because he won't tell me what's happening.

"If it was normal cartel business, the men you have watching me would be enough. You know that as well as I do. That means that there has to be something else going on."

He glances at me before peeling the skin off an onion. "I don't know what you want me to tell you."

"Don't play stupid with me, Jovan. It isn't a good look

on you. Why the hell am I here and why are you trying to control my life?"

"I'm making sure that you're safe."

"You're infuriating." I grab a slice of bell pepper and take a bite. "If you're going to keep secrets from me, then this is never going to work."

Maybe he's only keeping you close because you're having his baby. Maybe all his interest is in his heir.

It's a horrible thought, but it's one that's easy to consider with the way he is behaving right now. The thought plays over and over in my head as I wait for him to say something that gives me a little bit of clarity in this situation.

Jovan starts slicing up the onion, keeping his focus on the vegetable. "I lost my family to Felix Domingos. I killed his family to take control. I left him alive. He killed my family while my back was turned. I'm not going to let that happen a second time."

I nod and reach out to put my hand on his forearm. He glances at me, his mouth pressed into a thin line. After a moment, the tension in his shoulders eases.

"I just want to keep you safe. Felix is a dangerous man. He broke into your apartment when we were out of town. I don't know what he was looking for, but he did threaten to kill you."

My heart skips a beat. "Did you see the pictures from the ultrasound when the kitchen was packed up?"

The knife clatters to the counter as Jovan abandons everything to go sift through the boxes marked *kitchen*. He rips apart the boxes as I sit, completely frozen with terror.

"They're not here," he says, his voice sounding hollow as he looks over his shoulder at me.

My heart falls to my feet. "Shit."

"He knows about the baby."

As I stare at the mess surrounding Jovan, my hands start to shake. That ultrasound has been living on my fridge. It was my first glimpse of my baby and now it's gone. I hadn't even noticed it was missing over the last couple days. With all the other information and several lists I had put on my fridge, the ultrasound had gotten lost in a sea of papers.

And now it's with a man who wants to kill the people in Jovan's life.

If I wasn't falling for him, I would pack up and move to the other side of the country. I would tell him that all this shit wasn't worth it and then I wouldn't look back.

However, he has me in his grasp — mind, body, and soul. I knew it as soon as we got back from our weekend away. I saw a side to him that made me start to picture a future.

A future that I may never get.

"What are we going to do?" I ask, my hands shaking as I grip the edge of the counter and lean forward slightly. "He's going to come after us, isn't he?"

Jovan gets up from the floor and comes to stand between my legs. His big hands cup my face and he guides my head back until I'm looking at him.

"I'm going to do everything I can to protect you," he says, his thumbs drifting over my cheeks. "I'm going to make sure that Felix can't get to you. We're going to be okay. He might have the ultrasound, but that doesn't mean that he's going to do anything just yet."

Being here with Jovan is for the best. He's going to keep us safe. He's going to make sure that Felix can't get to the baby.

Although, Jovan is just one man. He may have a cartel at his back, but when it comes down to it, are they loyal enough to die for a woman he knocked up?

The thought of people dying for me does nothing to ease the panic that's bubbling to the surface.

"We're going to be okay," he says as his hands drop. His arms wrap around my waist and he pulls me into a hug that I think he needs just as much as I do. "I'm not going to let anything happen to you."

At that moment, I don't know whether he is talking to me or the baby.

I don't think I want to know.

Everybody else in my life has been nothing but disappointments. They let me down time and time again.

I don't want Jovan to be another one of those people but I don't know if there is any way to avoid it.

Have a little faith in him, the tiny voice in the back of my mind says. *He just might surprise you.*

18

JOVAN

Hadley leans back against the arm of the couch, her feet in my lap as a movie plays in the background. I rub her foot, pressing my thumbs into the muscles and easing away the aches she complains about after a long shift.

In the several days that she's lived with me, it's not often that she complains about anything.

She is taking the news of the man who wants to kill her better than I thought she would. Most people would have run the other way, but she is still around.

"Have you thought much about what happens once school starts back up?" I ask as I start to massage my way up her legs. I focus on the muscles of her calf as she sinks back into the cushions.

"I don't know. I'm going to go but I'm not going to be able to take much time off once the baby is born. I mean, I'll have the summer to be around but the baby is going to be here before I'm done for the year."

"Hadley, I'm able to take care of a baby while you go to your student teaching."

"I know. I'm going to talk to my advisor and see if I can

do it earlier in the year so I can take time off if I need to, though."

She moans as I rub a tight muscle, applying pressure to the knot that's built up there. I switch to her other leg, trying to keep my cock from standing at attention with the noises she's making.

"We're going to have the baby and work together as a team, Hadley. I have several businesses that I can run from home. I'm sure that Rio would be fine to step up and take over some of the operations for a little while."

In fact, I know that he would. He came to me only a short while ago about wanting to be more involved with the business. Rio has made it clear that he wants to make more money so he can give Kennedy the kind of life she deserves.

If anything were to ever happen to her, I don't think Rio would ever recover.

Just like I know I won't recover if anything happens to Hadley.

I don't know how she became as important as she did within such a short period of time, but she has. She's the reason I get up in the morning and hate life a little less. She makes me think that there is something worth living for beyond money and power.

For her, I would burn cities down and conquer the world.

Stepping back from my business and taking care of our child is nothing compared to that.

"Whatever you want to achieve in life, I want you to go after. I don't want you to hold yourself back because you're worried about who is going to care for the baby. We're in this together." I give her leg an affectionate squeeze.

"To be honest, I don't think I'm going to continue to work at the club either. I've made more than enough money from your bribes and generous tips to be able to afford school and cover all my expenses."

I roll my eyes and continue massaging her calf. "Hadley, there is no need for you to want for anything. If you don't have the money for something, let me know. I have more money than I know what to do with."

"I'm not going to just sit back and take your money." She gives me a flat look. "I'm not the kind of woman who is going to stick around just because you're paying her. I'm going to make a life for myself."

"I have no problem with you doing that. However, I can help make it easier. You won't have to worry about money and you can chase after whatever dreams you have."

Hadley's cheeks turn a slight shade of pink as she looks away from me. When she looks back at me, I can see a lingering suspicion in her eyes. Her gaze flits over me quickly, as if she can't believe what she is hearing.

I'm going to do everything in my power to make sure that she has everything she needs out of life.

I don't want her to feel like she's being held back because we're having a baby.

I'll do whatever I can to make sure she lives the life she wants.

Hell, if she left me tomorrow and said that she never wanted to see me again, it would kill me but I would let her go.

All I want is for her to be happy.

Who the hell am I becoming?

"Jovan, I appreciate the offer but I want to earn what I have. Owing a debt to the cartel is something that I'm going to avoid."

"It wouldn't be a debt," I say, slight irritation coloring my voice. "It would be me, helping the mother of my child."

Her lips press together in a thin line and she looks away from me. Hadley pulls her knees to her chest, putting distance between us.

I don't know what I said to upset her, but it's clear that I said something. "Hadley, if you want the money, it's there. If you want the connections to do whatever you want, they are there as well. I don't want you to feel trapped by this life."

"Yeah, well, it isn't always about what you want. I've done what you wanted from the moment we met. I might have given you hell about it, but I've done what you asked. I'm living here, even though I would much rather be in the home I worked for."

"Well, unlucky for you, this is your option right now," I say, my tone harsh as I stand. "If you want to earn the money, then I will offer you a bigger cut. You will be a partner instead of an employee."

"You always make our relationship sound entirely transactional." Hadley's eyes narrow. "Did you ever think that maybe the money and the connections don't matter to me at all? I thought I was just hooking up with some stranger at a club. Instead, it turned out to be my boss who manipulated me. Who knew exactly who I was and figured out what he could gain from the entire situation.

"Is that really what you think of me?" I shake my head as she gets to her feet and crosses her arms. "I might not be the best man and what I did when we first met was fucked up. I'm sorry, but right now, I'm trying to focus on what comes next for us."

"You know," she says, her hands dropping to her sides as if all the energy has been drained out of her. "*But* invalidates everything you said before that."

Before I have the chance to try and fix what has turned

into a terrible night, she walks away. I stand in the living room wondering how we got here.

You know how you got here. You keep pushing and pushing. You don't give her room to breathe. You become so focused on taking care of her that you refuse to let her be who she is.

I scowl as a door slams somewhere else in the house. For a moment, I consider going after her and trying to sort this out right now.

Instead, I send a message to one of the men guarding the house before gathering my keys, gun, and phone before heading out.

What I need right now is a walk in the cool night air to clear my head.

I nod to the men near the front door as I step outside. I shut and lock it before making my way to the street. The lights are shining bright against the night. I tilt my head back to look at the stars, though most of them are washed out by the light pollution in the city.

Staring at the sky in Miami isn't the same as sitting at the cabin and showing Hadley the constellations.

Cars pass by as I head for the gates of the community. The security guard on duty looks at me and nods before returning to the magazine he's reading. I stare at the little booth for a moment, wondering how a man with no formal training is going to take care of an entire gated community.

While the gate offers a certain level of security that other areas don't have, I still have my own men stationed throughout.

There is no such thing as being too careful.

I pass through the gates and head down the street. The lights of the downtown area are shining bright in the distance. I head in the opposite direction, needing some peace and quiet.

"You know, I've been wondering when you would step out of those little gates."

I turn around and see Felix hiding in the bushes. My hand drifts toward the gun in the back of my waistband.

"No need for weapons, Jovan. I'm just here to talk for now. We have a little catching up to do. After all, we haven't spoken since slaughtering each other's families."

"If you know what's best for you, you'll leave immediately. One shout from me and my men will come running."

The cold metal of a gun presses against my temple while a hand slips into my waistband and pulls out my gun. My heart hammers in my chest as I look at Felix.

I should have pulled the gun the moment I heard his voice. Not that it would have helped me. Based on the gun at my head, I would have been shot before I could pull the trigger.

"Now," Felix says, stepping out of the shadows with a grin. "We have some things to discuss."

Two men appear on either side of me while the gun presses harder against my head. I don't bother to fight as they restrain me. For all I know, Felix has someone watching Hadley. I don't want to risk doing something stupid and putting her in more danger.

"I don't want this to be an unpleasant conversation," Felix says as he tucks his hands into his pockets. "But I feel like there is some tension between the two of us we need to clear. You still seem to think that you run this town."

"What is the point of this?" I ask, my tone bored even though I know one misstep will put a bullet through my head.

"In case you haven't figured it out yet, Aguilar, I'm

going to be coming for you and your child. If you thought that killing your family ten years ago was all that I had planned for you, you would be sorely mistaken."

"You won't be touching my child. You won't live long enough."

Felix chuckles. "Cute. You really are stepping into the position of kingpin nicely. Unfortunately for you, I'm ready to retake the city. Deal with him, boys."

Something hard collides with the side of my head. I drop to the ground and more blows land to my body, all I have the presence of mind to do is protect my head the best I can.

WHEN I WAKE UP AFTER I DON'T KNOW HOW LONG, I'm alone in the street. I groan, my body aching as I get to my feet.

The second I'm standing, fear courses through me.

Hadley.

I take off back into my neighborhood, ignoring the pain that radiates through my body. All that matters is getting to her before Felix does.

If he hasn't already.

As I try to go faster, everything in my body hurts. None of it is important to me. I can rest once I know that she's okay. I have to make sure that she's still alive. Still safe. Still home.

I burst into the house. My head is spinning and I feel like I'm going to pass out.

Please be okay. I need you to be okay.

When I open the door to my bedroom, I try to prepare myself for the worst. I didn't see any of my men out front, but that doesn't mean anything. They might be circling the house.

Hadley has to be okay. Nothing has happened to her.

I flick on the light to the bedroom and Hadley groans. She rolls over and pulls her pillow over her face as a rush of relief runs through me.

As I cross the room to her, I bite back the tears that threaten to fall. While I ran here, I thought that I was going to be walking into my home to find a dead body.

I would have lost the best parts of myself if she was dead.

"Turn off the light please," she says, her voice muffled by her pillow.

"Sorry," I say, grinning as I look at her. "I just need to get cleaned up and I'll be right there."

She waves a hand at me before burying herself deeper into the blankets and the pillows. Holding my ribs due to the pain, I chuckle and turn off the light before heading into the washroom. As I close the door behind me, I hiss out a pained breath.

It takes a few moments of rummaging through the cabinets to find the pain medication. I take the dose and wash it down with some water before getting in the shower. The water runs through my bruised skin. My entire body feels tender, but all I can think about is getting into bed with Hadley.

After a few minutes, I step out of the shower and towel off. I look in the mirror and see the painting my body has become. Thankfully, my face remains unmarked.

Regardless, Felix is going to pay for this.

With a sigh, I turn off the lights and head to the bed. Hadley shuffles over to make room for me as I get in.

Even though I'm in pain, I need to hold her. I need to

know that she is safe in my arms and nobody is going to take her away from me. I loop an arm around her waist and pull her closer.

Despite our conversation earlier and the tension between us, she still rolls onto her side and cuddles against me.

My heart races as I hold her close. She sighs and nestles against me. The feeling of her body pressed against mine combined with the pain medication slowly starting to work is enough to make me feel a bit better.

Even though the ache continues through my body as she presses against me, I'm not going to ask her to move away. Not after the shit I've been through tonight.

"We're not done talking about all of this shit," she says as she puts her hand on my chest. "I don't want to fight anymore tonight."

Cocooned by the darkness around her, I kiss the top of her head. "Nothing about us is transactional, Hadley. I'll sit back and allow you to take the lead from now on."

She laughs and kisses me. "I believe you mean that, but you know the two of us are going to be constantly fighting each other for control. We're too broken not to. Being in control is what we've both had to do to survive."

We might be broken, but every day I spend with her, I feel those little shattered pieces starting to glue themselves back together.

19

HADLEY

WALKING INTO UNIVERSITY WITH TWO CARTEL members flanking me isn't how I want to start my school year. I thought that Jovan would back off a little once school started, but he is still sending his people with me everywhere I go.

"I don't suppose either of you would like to take the day off?" I say as a couple girls I have classes with look at me and start whispering to each other. "I don't think that I need the two of you following me around."

"Not going to happen," Rio says, grinning as he looks at me. "You know as well as I do that nobody is going to defy the boss."

"You do."

Rio shrugs. "It depends on the matter. When it comes to your safety, I'm not going to disobey him."

I groan and look around. More people are looking at me. I don't know what they think and I try to convince myself that it doesn't matter anyway. They don't know that I'm pregnant and they don't know who these men are.

The other students might be looking at me, but they don't know what's going on with my life.

That's what I try to tell myself even though the darker part of my brain insists that strangers know everything.

How the hell am I supposed to do this? To finish my education with cartel members following me around and a baby on the way.

I can't do this.

"Give us a minute," Rio says to the other man, jerking his chin in the direction of a bench.

The other man looks at me for a moment before nodding and walking away. Rio waits until the man is out of earshot before stepping in front of me. He crosses his arms and looks down.

"Hadley, whatever is going through your head right now isn't as bad as you're making it." Rio grins and shakes his head when I start to open my mouth. "Save it, Hadley. You might be able to talk circles around Jovan, but Kennedy is a lot like you. She gets the same look on her face when she is trapped in her own head and overthinking."

I heft my laptop bag higher up on my shoulder. "I don't know what to tell you. I have a lot going on in my life and then there is this on top of it."

"I get it. I really do. I know that this is a lot for anyone to handle, but the truth is that you are in danger. If allowing us to follow you around all day means that you are going to be that much safer, then stop worrying."

"Rio, I'm scared."

He offers me a soft smile. "I know. Jovan is scared too. It doesn't excuse how he acts, but it is an explanation. I was with him when his family died. He's never dealt with that pain. He's going to tighten control now that you're in danger."

"I know I'm going to have to deal with some of his protectiveness, but I think this is a bit much."

"Yeah," Rio says, sarcasm dripping from his tone. "Because murders — especially in a crime-filled city — don't happen anywhere at any time."

My cheeks warm and I lower my eyes to my shoes. "You're right."

"I know I am." He lifts my head up with a finger curled under my chin and gives me a toothy grin. "Now, hold your head high and let's go to class. If you don't give a shit what other people think about you, you'll have a much better day."

I nod and the other man joins us. He doesn't say anything as he follows me to class.

There has to be more to the rest of my life than this.

WHEN I GET HOME LATER THAT NIGHT, JOVAN IS standing in the hallway, nearly bouncing up and down. His grin stretches from one side of his face to the other. A sinking feeling appears in the pit of my stomach as guilt claws at me.

I was planning on walking in here and trying to argue with him about having two people follow me around all day. I was going to see if he would lower it to one person.

When he looks this happy to see me, it kills any thought I have about trying to alter the agreement because I know he is just trying to keep me safe. I want my baby to be safe. He knows more about what Felix is capable of than I do.

It's time to stop fighting Jovan every step of the way. I just need to let him take control in this one area of my life. It's not just me he is protecting, but our baby too.

"Hey," he says, reaching out to take my bag from me. "I've been working on something that I want to show you."

He puts the bag in the home office he deemed as mine before linking his fingers with mine and towing me down the hall. I smile, trying to enjoy whatever he is about to show me even though I feel terrible.

"What do you think?" Jovan asks as he opens one of the doors across the hall from his bedroom.

I step inside the room and that sinking feeling only intensifies. "What is this?"

"I got the nursery together."

As I stare at the nursery, I try not to cry. I bite back the tears as hard as I can as I look around at the light wood furniture and the pale sage walls. The window is open to air out the smell of drying paint.

"What is this?" I ask, my voice hollow as my chest constricts.

"I saw you looking at some of this stuff while we were in bed last night. I thought that I could get it and set the nursery up while you were at school."

He beams at me like he's given me the best surprise in the world. I feel like shit for feeling as if I've been robbed of something. Jovan is trying to do something nice and he picked out everything I like.

"This is beautiful." It feels like I'm choking on the words.

"What's wrong?" he asks, his eyebrows knitting together as he looks down at me. "Do you not like it? If this isn't what you wanted to do, then I can return it all and we can figure something else out."

I take a deep breath and try to find the words to explain everything that is going through my mind. This is just one more thing to pile onto all the ways that I feel like my life has been invaded.

There is no privacy in my life anymore. No safety. No time to figure things out on my own and work for what I want.

I know that Jovan means well, but it is a lot to process.

"I like it and I really do appreciate the effort you went to. It's beautiful. I just thought that I would have been involved with setting up the baby's nursery. I thought that I would get to be there for the shopping and the painting."

Jovan's smile falls completely. "Fuck. Hadley, I'm sorry. I honestly thought that this was a surprise that you would like. I never would have overstepped if I had stopped to think about how important this was for you."

"It's okay," I say, though my voice cracks a little. "The last few days have been a lot to process, though. Everything about my life has changed and it feels like you're the one in control."

"I don't want to control you, Hadley."

Tears burn my eyes as I nod. "I know you don't. At least, that's what I'm working on coming to terms with. It's difficult. I've relied on myself for so long that having someone else who gives a shit is hard to wrap my head around."

Jovan sighs and looks around at the room. "I'm going to paint it white again tomorrow and remove everything. Whenever you're ready, we can go shopping for everything together."

Some of the tightness in my chest starts to ease. I feel like I'm getting a little bit of control back in my life. Even if it is just this tiny amount, I appreciate it.

"Thank you," I say. "I really do love the color you got for the walls, though. Why don't we keep it that color?"

Jovan smiles at me, his entire face lighting up again. It's

nice to see that he is excited about the baby, even if it brings a thousand different fears surging to the surface.

My baby isn't even through the first trimester and I already have to accept the fact that their life is going to be forever connected to the cartel.

I just have to make sure that I don't fall into the same shit that my parents did.

20

JOVAN

Hadley takes off her heels as we stand at the edge of the dock. I reach out a hand to help her onto the yacht before hopping on after her. She grins as she looks around, the warm breeze blowing through her hair.

"If I had known that you owned a yacht, I would have asked to come out here sooner," she says as she climbs the stairs to the upper deck.

"I don't make a habit of going around and announcing that I have a yacht. People start wanting to party on the yacht and that makes it hard to impress a beautiful woman with a night alone."

Her cheeks turn a bright pink as we reach the upper deck. The captain nods to me as he disappears inside the boat.

"Where are we going to head tonight?" she asks as she sits down on one of the lounge chairs and tucks her heels underneath.

I take off my own shoes and put them beneath my chair. "I think the captain is going to give us a tour of the coast. The chef is going to be making some food too."

Hadley nods and leans back in the chair, looking up at the stars as the crew start to untie the yacht from the dock. "It's a beautiful night to spend some time out on the water."

"Even if it wasn't, the view from the bedroom is pretty great," I say as I pull my chair closer to hers before sitting down.

Hadley laughs and shakes her head, her eyes sparkling in the dim light. "You really are something else, aren't you?"

"I like to think that I'm a man who knows what he wants."

"And what do you want?" she asks, her tone teasing as I reach out and take her hand.

I lace our fingers together and kiss the back of her hand. "I think I've made it clear by now that I want you. Shit isn't easy between us but I wouldn't want it any other way. I like that you make me work for your affection."

"I don't make you work too hard, do I?"

Smiling, I kiss the back of her hand again. "I wouldn't be interested if you weren't hard on me. Not a lot of people have the balls to stand up to me the way you do. Hell, Rio is the only one who comes close most days and even he has a limit. Not you, though. You tell me to go fuck myself with the same mouth you wrap around my cock."

Her cheeks turn a violent shade of red as one of the crew appears with glasses of sparkling apple juice. The steward clears his throat and sets down the drinks before spinning and walking away.

"Well, at least that's likely not the worst thing he's heard while working for you."

"Wouldn't know. You're the only woman I've ever brought on a solo trip here."

The smile that she gives me is worth all the hell that we've gone through in the last few weeks and all the shit that we have yet to go through. I know that it's only a matter of time before Felix makes a move and tries to take her from me.

Then there is the matter of her connection to the Domingos cartel. I still don't know what it is and there is a very large part of me that never wants to find out.

"This is delicious," Hadley says after taking a sip of her juice. "Just under seven more months and we could do this again but with champagne."

Warmth spreads through me at the mention of a future between us. It makes me happy to know that I'm not the only one thinking about what is going to come after the baby.

I want her for as long as she is willing to let me have her.

"Alright," I say as I settle into the chair and cross one leg over the other. "Tell me about everything you want to achieve in your life."

Hadley barks out a laugh before taking another sip of her drink. "Just like that, you want to know everything?"

"We're going to have a child together. We've spent a lot of time talking but you never say much about where you're going or where you've come from. I want to know everything there is to know about you, no matter how insignificant you may find it."

She swirls her juice around in her glass. "It's not that I think it's insignificant. It's more that I think it will scare people away. You already know I lived in my car and took care of myself in a house full of addicts. There's not much more to my past than that."

"I think there's a lot more than that to your story."

"I knew how to call the ambulance for an overdose before I went to kindergarten," she says, a hint of bitterness in her voice. "My mother stopped cooking for me once I was big enough to stand on a chair and do it myself without setting the house on fire."

"How old were you then?"

"Seven."

My chest constricts as I think about a young Hadley fending for herself. All the adults in her life failed her. They should have been there, taking care of her. Someone should have seen what was going on and taken her out of that home.

"I don't think my parents even really loved me. I think that I just happened to be born and they realized that there was someone to clean the house and make them food when they were too high to do it for themselves."

"Did you ever get removed from the home?" I ask, getting up and motioning her forward on the chair.

Hadley moves forward slightly and I squeeze myself in behind her. My legs bracket hers on the wide lounger. She leans back against my chest with a sigh as my arms wrap around her.

"No. The teachers knew what was going on — how could you not when I showed up to school with matted hair and dirty clothes? When I begged for any food that I could get? They knew, but they didn't do anything to help me."

"And that's why you want to be a teacher."

She nods and tilts her head back on my shoulder to look up at me. "I told you that before but I think it's more than that too. I want to give kids the love they might not be getting from home but I want to save them all too. I don't know what's going to happen when a day comes and I can't."

"I'll be there to help. In whatever way you need it. You want to cry, we can cry. If you want me to pull every connection I have to intervene in something dangerous, I'll do it."

She studies me for a moment, her eyes widening in surprise. "You really mean that, don't you?"

"Yes." I kiss her temple. "I told you that I was going to do whatever I could to help you with your dreams. You say the word and I can make things happen. Anything, really."

"It's easy to forget how much power you have in this city." Hadley glances back out over the water. "I don't want our child to go through the same shit that I did. It's why I don't want them involved with the cartel. I want to give them the best shot at life possible."

I sigh and tighten my embrace around her. "I know. I don't want them to be as deep into the life as I am either. I want our child to benefit from the money and the power, but this isn't the life that I would choose for anyone."

"Then why are you in it?"

"I didn't have anything else going for me. I was already in the Domingos cartel, but there was unrest. I was young at the time and I had a chip on my shoulder. Thought that I had something to prove so when the chance came to take power, I took it. I did a lot of things that I'm not proud of, and it got my family killed."

Her breath hitches slightly and for a moment I think that I might have said too much. She knows that my family was murdered. I have no doubt that she knows the things I did to take power.

I'm not proud of it. What I did back then was horrible. I had nothing to lose and I made sure that everyone knew it.

"Do you ever wish that you could go back in time and change it all?"

I tilt my head back to look at the stars shining overhead. "Yes and no. I wish that so many innocent people didn't die.

I wish that my family was still alive. Both things would be true if I didn't take control."

"Then why wouldn't you go back in time and change it, if that were possible?"

"Everything that I've ever done in my life has led me to this moment with you and our child. If I were to go back and change just one thing, I would have never met you. I wouldn't have gotten to experience the light that you bring into my life or the way you don't take my shit."

She nestles against me as my fingers trail along her hip. "You know, I used to think that if I could just go back in time and make one teacher speak up and say something, that my life would have turned out a lot better."

"And now what do you think?"

"I think that meeting you might have been the best mistake of my life."

I grin and kiss her, getting lost in the feeling of her mouth on mine as we leave the business of Miami behind. Out here, nothing can touch us. I don't have to worry about Felix or that Hadley is going to get up and walk away.

Right now, she is safe in my arms and I couldn't think of a better way to spend my night.

Of course, that all comes crashing down an hour later when my phone vibrates with a text as Hadley is in the washroom. I groan and pull the phone out of my pocket, wishing that I could ignore it. As I unlock the phone, I head to the railing to look out at the waves.

Rio: **The Brazen is burning. Felix is suspect #1. Come quick.**

"Fuck!" I send Rio a quick reply before telling the steward to ask the captain to turn around.

Right now, I would like nothing more than to throw my phone into the water and pretend I never got the message.

However, that would be a sign of weakness. Those in Miami who are wavering with their allegiance to me will see ignoring the fire as a clear message that I am losing power in my own city.

Like fuck I'm going to let that happen.

The steward is in the middle of scurrying away when Hadley appears on the deck again with a bright smile. I try to force a smile back at her, but my pulse is pounding and anger is boiling to the surface.

Felix Domingos is a dead man walking.

"Is everything alright?" Hadley loops her arms around my waist and leans her head into my chest.

I kiss the top of her head and run a hand up and down her bare back. "No. We have to head back to the marina. The Brazen has been set on fire and Rio is certain that Felix is behind it."

Hadley stiffens and looks up at me. I see a million different emotions flicker across her face before she unwraps her arms and turns away from me. And I hate the cold I feel from her distance. We were having a good night. Of course Felix would find a way to ruin this for us.

"Alright, well, I guess we're going to have to do dessert another time," she says as she turns back to me with a smile. "Are you okay?"

"You're asking me if I'm okay?" I laugh and shake my head, pulling her back to me. "Hadley, I'm fine. I'm just worried about ruining your night. I was trying to make this something special for us and then shit like this has to happen."

"You'll handle it," she says, standing on her toes to kiss me softly.

Rio is standing across the road from The Brazen when we arrive. I step out of the car and join him while Hadley sits in the passenger seat and scrolls through her phone. Rio casts her a worried glance before looking at me.

Alessio gets out of another car and walks over to us, looking at the burning building before turning to me. "You got here fast."

"I didn't know you were back in town," I say as I look at him. "I thought that you liked me enough to tell me when you were coming to pay me a visit."

Alessio shrugs and smiles. "I heard that Felix was planning something big through the grapevine. Thought you might need a little more help when it came to him. My consigliere is watching over my people until I get back. I have a few of the men I still trust with me."

I nod. "Thank you for coming. I could use the extra support right now. I don't know what is going to happen with Felix, but the more people we have in the city watching for him, the better."

"How is she taking this? I know that everything is more than she bargained for right now." Alessio looks at me before turning his attention to Hadley.

I don't miss the glimmer in Rio's eyes as they narrow. It's the same look he gets when someone upsets Kennedy. He is the kind of man who will stand up to anyone and anything for the people he's loyal too.

Yet another person on the list that outranks me in his eyes.

Although, I'm not upset about it. Knowing that Rio is going to put Hadley above nearly everything else makes me feel better.

"She is coping. Right now I'm going to be taking her home and locking her in. Rio, I want you to follow us and stay there with her. Bring Kennedy too. Hadley could use a friend right now."

"You don't want me to track down Felix?" Rio asks, looking over at Alessio. "He could stay with them while I go out and hunt."

I shake my head and look at the flames climbing higher up the side of my club even as the firefighters try to douse them. "No. I want you with her. You are the person I trust to look after her. Others will be there but I question their loyalty to the job."

"Easy enough ways to test that," Rio says, his voice gruff as he looks back at Hadley. "I'll pick up Kennedy and meet you at your house."

"Thank you."

Alessio looks at me as Rio disappears down the street. "So, Hadley, she's it for you, huh?"

"It sounds strange to admit, but yeah." I swallow the lump that rises in my throat. "I don't know what I'm going to do if anything happens to her."

"You're going to get your shit together and keep going, even though it's going to hurt like hell." Alessio reaches out to clap me on the shoulder. "Look, I don't want to see you get hurt the way my mother did when my father died. She still hasn't been able to pull herself together. I don't want that for you."

I study him for a moment, noticing the distant look in his eyes. "Is that why you're still alone after all this time?"

Alessio frowns, tucking his hands into his pockets. "We're not talking about me and my love life right now."

"So, there is one to talk about?" I try to keep my tone light and teasing, but I feel sick to my stomach. I need Hadley to get through this mess with Felix without getting hurt.

Knowing that she will be his target and being unable to hunt him down before he gets to her is killing me inside.

He's out there somewhere, waiting for the right moment to strike like the other night when he ambushed me. He'll die waiting if it's up to me.

"Love is for people who like pain. I'm not one of those people. I've witnessed what it does to people when it ends or when you lose your loved one and I'm not sure I could take a hit like that now. Not when I'm already doing something I was never meant to do."

"Sorry about that. No one expected you'd lose your dad and your brother so close to one another," I say, holding his gaze with my own. "Whatever you need once we're done with the Felix thing, you got it."

He nods to some of his men standing off in the shadows. "I'll start looking for Felix. Sooner or later, we're going to be able to drag him out from whatever rock he's crawled under."

"I really do appreciate you coming out here. I know that you have enough going on back home."

"It's being handled and you need help. I'm not about to turn my back on you."

"Are you sure? I can sure use the help, but I'll handle this if you need to be back in Atlanta."

Alessio shakes his head. "Right here is where I need to be. The situation back home isn't good, but it's stable enough for now. Keeping my friend alive is more important than the mafia anyway."

"Your father would hate to hear you say that," I say, the corner of my mouth turning upward slightly. "I'm glad that you're nothing like him."

"Me too." He sighs and nods in Hadley's direction.

"You should go take care of your woman, loverboy. I'm going to go join the search."

"Alright. Thank you."

Alessio takes off while I get back in the car with Hadley. She looks at me, a thin line appearing between her eyebrows as she tucks a strand of hair behind her ear.

"Is everything alright?" she asks as she reaches over to turn down the music. "The two of you looked pretty serious."

"I'm going to be taking you to the house where I know you'll be safe. I asked Rio to go get Kennedy so you aren't completely alone."

Her smile is enough to make my heart beat against my ribcage. "Thank you for that. I wasn't going to say anything but I don't really want to be surrounded by a bunch of strangers while there's some man that wants to kill me on the loose."

I start the engine and head in the direction of home. "I want you to grab a gun from the safe when you get home. One for Kennedy too. Rio is going to be stationed inside with both of you while I have other men outside. The security system will be armed but in the event that something does happen, I need to know that you are able to take care of yourself."

Hadley takes my hand, her thumb smoothing over the back of it. "Everything is going to be okay, Jovan."

As I drop her off at home, I'm not so sure about that.

"Stay safe," Hadley says, her voice wavering as I finish setting the security system.

"I will." I kiss her quickly before reaching up to swipe away a tear. "Everything is going to be alright. I doubt we'll even find Felix tonight. This was just a pathetic show to make it clear to everyone that he isn't interested in backing down from a fight."

"You promise me that you're going to come back home, Jovan. Show or not."

I wrap her in a tight hug and bury my face in her hair. "I promise that I'm going to come back home to you, Hadley. You don't have to worry about me. I know how to handle myself. I promise."

As I step away from her and head outside, I know it's a promise that I never should have made and one that I desperately want to keep.

21

HADLEY

"Is she asleep?" Jovan asks from somewhere within the house. His voice carries down the hall to our room.

I yawn as I sit up in bed. Rio mumbles a reply but he isn't speaking loud enough for me to hear.

After a moment, Jovan stumbles into our bedroom. He leans against the wall and crosses his arms while I reach over and turn on the light.

The air is stolen from my lungs as I get a good look at him. Cuts cover his arms and face. Blood stains his skin. He looks like he's been in the fight of his life, though knowing him, it wasn't.

"Are you okay?" I ask as I get out of bed and race across the room to him. "Where are you still bleeding? Do we need to go to the hospital? Damn it, Jovan. You can't just come home looking like you crawled through a murder scene."

"Hadley, I'm alright. There's a bullet in my arm that I'm going to need you to pull out, but other than that, I'm fine."

"What the fuck, Jovan! You can't just come home and

tell me that there is a bullet lodged in your arm like it is nothing. Holy shit. Get to the bathroom before you bleed all over the floor and stain it."

He laughs and shakes his head. "Glad to see that your concern is over the floor and not the man who lets you steal his blankets every night."

"You're the dumbass who decided to go get shot," I say as I follow him into the bathroom. My face softens a little as he sits on the edge of the tub. "You are alright, aren't you?"

"I'm going to be just fine, kitten, I promise. Now, do you know how to pull a bullet out or is it something I'm going to need to walk you through?"

I scowl and start rummaging through the drawers. "I know how to pull a bullet out. I can't say that I'm happy to have to do that now, though. What happened to you? Are you alright? And don't give me some bullshit answer to keep me from worrying."

He chuckles and grabs the hem of my shorts, pulling me over to him even though I'm still digging around for the long tweezers I saw earlier. I sigh and give up, letting his gentle tugging lead me over to him.

Jovan takes my hand and kisses the back of it. "I'm okay, Hadley. I promise that I am. It's nothing that hasn't happened before. As for what happened, well, Carlos was waiting for us. Said that I should stop digging. One of my guys went to put him down but we were ambushed by Felix's men."

"Did everyone on your side get out alive?" I kiss his cheek before going back to the drawers. Finally, I find the tweezers and everything else I need to take out the bullet. "I think this is going to need stitches too."

"I have a medical kit with everything you need to stitch

me up. If you're not comfortable doing that, I have a doctor on staff." Jovan groans as he moves his arm a little too quickly. "No. Not everybody on *our* side made it out alive."

I shake my head as he strips his shirt off and reveals the bullet wound. As I dab away the blood with a wet cloth so I can see what I'm doing, Jovan hisses in pain. I sigh and try to be gentler, but I need most of the blood cleaned away before I pull the bullet out of his arm.

"Is there anything I can do for their families?" I ask as I swipe away the last of the blood on his arm. The wound is still bleeding but it's slowed down enough for me to try and get the bullet out.

"Hadley, you don't have to do anything. Their families will be compensated for everything."

I shake my head and hand him a rolled up cloth to bite down on. "I don't mean giving them money. I mean helping them out. Making meals for them. Taking care of the children if they need a night out."

"They're going to be fine." He puts the cloth in his mouth and bites down.

"You don't know that," I say as I tie my hair back into a ponytail. "You don't know anything that is going to happen. These people now have to survive without the other person that was taking care of the family. The least I can do is offer a little bit of support for the next few weeks."

Jovan's breath hitches as I shine the flashlight from my phone at the wound while holding his arm still. I lighten my grip a little but keep looking for the bullet. As soon as I see it, I grab the tweezers.

My heart is racing as I insert the tweezers. I hold my breath as I poke around for a second before the tweezers close around the bullet. More blood is seeping out of the wound as I pull the bullet out and drop it into the sink.

He spits the cloth out and closes his eyes. His teeth grind together for a moment as I wipe my hands on a towel. While I dab at the blood on his arm, my stomach starts to toss and turn. I take a deep breath, trying not to get sick over the thought of what I just did.

"The other medical supplies are in my closet. Top drawer in the dresser."

I nod and head to his closet, digging through unmatched socks until I find the little medical kit. When I walk back into the bathroom, Jovan is cleaning the blood from his face. His lip is swollen and dark circles are beneath his eyes.

He looks like he's been sleeping as much as I have through this entire process.

"Hadley," he says as I put the medical kit on the counter and open it up. "Your hands are shaking. Are you alright?"

I take another deep breath, my heart thudding against my chest. The needle twitches in my hand, even as I try to put the thread through the eye.

"Hadley." His tone is stern as he takes the needle from my hand. "You don't need to stitch me up right this second. Take a minute to tell me what is wrong. I don't want any other ugly scars."

Despite the panic that keeps rolling through me in waves, I laugh and put the thread down. "I don't know where to start."

"At the beginning is usually a good place."

I run my hand through my hair. "I don't know. I keep thinking that I'm going to be like my parents."

"You're not a drug addict."

"No, but where do you think I learned to take bullets out of people?" My chest constricts a little. "My dad was shot once or twice. Maybe more than that. I honestly don't remember. They used to get me to pull the bullet out because my fingers were small. I could get in there better than the tweezers could. Now look at me. I'm still doing the same kind of shit, just with a man far more dangerous than the two of them ever were."

"Do you honestly think I would do anything to hurt you, Hadley? Because if you do, then I think we need to think long and hard about where this relationship is going."

"No. I don't think that you would hurt me but I do think I'm in over my head. I'm hanging around the cartel and I know they did too. I keep thinking that being near the cartel is what's going to ruin my life the way it ruined theirs."

Jovan grabs my hand and pulls me to him. He pulls me down until I'm sitting on his knee. As I gently perch there, he wraps an arm around my waist.

"I knew your parents. At least, I knew of them. They came to me once and asked for a forgiveness of their debt."

I swallow hard. "Did they get their debt forgiven?"

Jovan gives me a sad look. "Nobody gets their debt forgiven. Especially not then. I had only been in charge of the cartel for a couple of years at that point. I couldn't seem weak, no matter how much they begged. I had to make sure that people knew I wasn't a person to fuck over or take advantage of."

I don't know what to think about that or how to process it. Jovan's hand drifts up and down my side as he kisses my shoulder.

"That was the second time that they came to me. It was the last time that I saw them before their death. To be honest, I had forgotten about them for a long time. They were just two other drug addicts in a long line of others looking to get more drugs for less."

My breath hitches and I get up from his lap. My hands

are still shaking as I grab the cloth and wipe away the rest of the blood that is starting to pool on his arm.

"Hadley, the first time they saw me, they wanted a loan. I gave it to them. They told me they had a daughter that they needed to support. Showed me your picture."

I bite back the tears that threaten to fall as I put down the cloth and grab the needle. "I don't know what to say to that. To be honest, I don't know what your point is. The only time that they gave a shit about me was when they needed me for something. The second I was done being useful to them, I stopped mattering."

"The point is that you are nothing like your parents. Not even a little bit. You don't come to the cartel asking for shit. You could have asked me for money for your schooling at any point and I would have happily handed it over. Instead, you worked for everything you have."

I thread the needle and take another deep breath before starting to stitch shut the wound. "I don't know about that. Sometimes when I look in the mirror, I can see glimpses of them. The harder parts of me are them."

"No," he says, wincing when I pull the needle through a little too tight. "The harder parts of you are you. They are what happened when you survived the shit you had to go through. They made you who you are and they made you the kind of woman who is going to make sure that our baby has the best life possible."

The first tear slips down my cheek as I finish stitching him up. "Thank you for that."

"I mean it, Hadley. When I think about having a baby with you, I think about how lucky that baby is going to be. They get to be loved by you and that's the best thing that could ever happen."

I wipe away the rest of the blood and smile, even as my vision blurs from the tears. "Thank you for saying that."

"Come on," Jovan says as he stands up. "I could use a shower to get the rest of the blood off. You could help me and count my bruises."

"I did that the last time you were beat up." I couldn't even believe it when I saw him that morning. How had he even gotten home by himself is beyond me. I'm shaking my head. He'd gotten into bed with me after our fight and hadn't uttered a single word about his pain, while he held me all night long. This man can surprise me in ways I can't even imagine. "I'm not sure I want to do that again," I say, kissing his cheek as I gather the bloody supplies. "What do you want done with this?"

He gives me a sheepish smile. "We're going to have to burn it."

With a nod, I dump everything into the garbage can. "It can be burned in the morning. Why don't you get yourself cleaned up and then we can go back to bed."

Jovan gives me a quick kiss. "I won't be long."

As he showers, I clean the blood off my hands before backtracking to the front door and cleaning up the blood he left behind. By the time I finish cleaning, Jovan is leaning back against the pillows, his bare chest making my mouth water.

"You're looking at me like I'm a piece of meat," he says, amusement in his tone as he lifts the blanket and motions for me to get in.

I'm grinning as I get into bed beside him and lean into his embrace. Jovan smells like his musky soap as I put my head on his shoulder.

"Do you ever think that we have no business raising a

baby?" I ask, my voice wavering slightly. "I don't think that I'm ready at all."

"I don't think that anybody is ever ready to have a baby. Not even when they're on their second or third baby. I don't think there is any way to get ready for a human who is going to spend their day shitting and vomiting on you."

As I laugh, some of the tension leaves my body. Jovan always seems to know what to say to make me feel better. It's as if nothing can get under his skin.

"I'm scared."

He kisses my temple. "I am too. We would be stupid not to be."

"Are you worried about the baby being near the cartel? I'm terrified of that. You seem to be a lot calmer than I am about it."

"I'm not calm about it at all." His arm tightens around me as my heart starts to race. "I know about all the risks that could come from us having a child. I'm not stupid enough to think that everything is going to be fine. But I do know that you and the baby are safer with me than you are without me."

I sigh and nestle closer into his side. "How can you keep us safe from everything?"

"I can't."

It's that simple admission that makes me think we're going to be able to do this together. He isn't as unphased and calm about everything as I think he is. No, he's just as scared as I am.

There is comfort in knowing that.

"You're going to be a great mother, Hadley. I know that getting pregnant wasn't something either of us planned for, but I can't tell you how excited I am that someday soon we're going to have a baby of our own."

"I can't wait either."

He grins and holds me closer, his hand drifting up and down my side.

It's the normalcy of the moment as we talk about our futures that has me thinking everything is going to be okay between us.

One way or another, we're going to make everything work.

22

JOVAN

HADLEY SINGS ALONG WITH THE MUSIC SOFTLY playing in the background as she crouches over what will be the crib. There are a dozen different pieces scattered around the beige area rug in front of her. Her eyebrows are pulled together as she stares down at the instructions.

"How's it going over there?" I ask as I put the last bolt in the rocking chair and tighten it. "You look like you're ready to throw everything away."

"I should have just kept the furniture that you bought," she says, looking up at me. The corner of her mouth tips upward and she winks before turning back to the instructions.

"I like the things you picked out better. It matches more. I picked too many things that clashed with each other. I have no taste."

At that, Hadley cracks up, her eyes sparkling as she shakes her head. "You're so full of shit. I picked out all of that stuff too. You just ordered it."

I grin. "Well, I've got this together. Do you want me to help or do you want me to build the changing table?"

"I can handle this." Hadley flips the instructions upside down. "Maybe."

As I look at her, I can see the future with her. I can see us with more children. Our children grown up and their children playing around our feet. One day, I could see us retired and living on a ranch in the middle of nowhere, leaving everything about the past behind us.

With her, I see forever starting to play itself out in front of me.

"Come on," I say, standing up and stretching instead of opening the changing table box. "Let's go take a break and then we can finish the rest of this damn furniture."

I hold out my hand to her and she takes it. Her hand is soft against mine as I pull her to her feet. She smiles as her fingers twine with mine and I lead her out into the backyard.

"What do you think about building a treehouse?" I ask, nodding to one of the big trees in the far corner of the yard.

"I think that we need to build a fence around the pool first. I don't want to risk the baby falling in. And as soon as they're old enough, I want the baby in swimming lessons."

I grin and drop her hand to sit on one of the loungers. I pat the space between my legs and she obliges, sitting down and leaning back into my chest. I kiss her shoulder, the sun beating down from above.

It's a beautiful day and I'm sitting in my backyard with a woman who made my entire world mean something more.

"I love you," I say as I drop another kiss to her shoulder. "I love you, and it terrifies me and excites me at the same time. You came into my life and it changed everything for me. Which terrifies me. I don't want to lose you the way I lost the rest of my family."

Hadley turns in my arms and straddles my lap. She

cups my face with her hands, her fingers drifting across my cheeks. I smile up at her, though my heart is racing in my chest.

"I love you too," she says, her voice barely more than a whisper. "And I'm scared as hell about what that means for our lives."

I tuck a strand of hair behind her ear, my smile stretching across my face. "Well, at least that means that we're in this together. We're going to have to talk about what that means for the rest of our lives, though, because I don't want anyone else. I'm going to marry you one day, when all this shit is over, and I have time to give you the wedding and the honeymoon of your dreams."

"You didn't even ask if I wanted to marry you." Hadley laughs and kisses me, our mouths moving softly and slowly as we try to prolong the moment for as long as possible. "I love you so damn much. I didn't know it was possible to fall for someone this hard."

"Hadley, when I ask you, I'm going to ask you properly. Right now, I'm just letting you know that I don't plan on spending another day without you in my life. Especially one where you don't know what you mean to me."

The sun is starting to set as she gives me the smile that makes time seem to stop. Her eyes shine in the dimming light. All that I want out of life is right here in my arms.

"Sometimes, I feel like all this is going to slip away from me," I say as I pull her a little closer to me. Her hands glide over my shoulders, her touch making me feel like my nerves have been set on fire.

"I'm not going anywhere. You told me that you're in love with me. That means you're stuck with me now. Nothing you're going to be able to do about it." She smooths a finger over a wrinkle on my forehead. "What's got you worried?"

"I wasn't able to protect my parents and my sister. I let myself relax for a moment too long and then they were all taken from me. Sometimes, I think about going back in time and changing everything I did then."

"I know what you mean, and yet I still think we were right the last time we talked about that. If you went back and changed everything, you would be missing out on a lot of what happened." She pushes some of my hair back from my face. "I think that everything in life happens for a reason, even if we don't know what that reason is until many years down the road."

"I don't know if there is a reason for a loss like that." I sigh and lean my head against her shoulder. "I don't know how I'm going to keep you and the baby safe when I couldn't even keep my family safe over a decade ago. Felix has had eleven years to think about what he is going to do to fuck up my family."

"You're not in this alone, Jovan. We're a team. You're going to teach me to fight and shoot better. I'm going to be able to defend myself. I don't need you to save me. I need you to allow me to be your partner."

"And what if I can't do that?" I look up at her and the world around us seems to fade into the background. My pulse pounds in my veins as my stomach lurches. "Sometimes I think that locking you up would be the best option for keeping you safe."

"I would find a way out." She kisses me softly again. "I love you. Let me help you. Let me past all the walls that you throw up to keep yourself safe. I want to help you protect our family. Neither of us has to be on our own anymore."

The thought of anything happening to her or our baby

makes me feel sick. I want to refuse her but I know Hadley is the kind to keep pushing and fighting. It's what drew me to her in the first place and it's what made me fall head over heels for her.

She has a fire inside her that burns bright enough to eclipse the sun and warm the coldest of hearts.

After all, she did warm mine.

"Together, then," I say as I run my hands up and down her waist. "But if at any point you decide that you want to walk away from it all, I'm not going to stop you."

"Why would you say that?" Hadley asks.

"Because I love you too much to ever force you to stay. I know you have your reservations about raising our baby in the cartel and I have my own. If you have to leave, then I won't hold you back. All I want for you is to be happy and safe."

Hadley's eyes fill with tears and she nods. "If I get to a point where I think I have to go, then I'll go. We're safe right now, though. At least, as safe as we can be."

"I'm nothing if not prepared for the future," I say, my fingers weaving through her hair.

I pull her down for a kiss, trying to pour everything I feel for her into it. I want her to know how much I love her and how willing I am to walk to the ends of the world for her.

I want Hadley to be happy and while I hope she's happy with me, I'm not naive enough to think that everything between us is going to work out perfectly.

I love her like hell, though, and I'm going to fight for her and for us every step of the way.

There is nobody else I would rather have by my side for the rest of my life.

"I love you," I say, kissing my way down her neck as my hands slip beneath her shirt.

As I pull the silky material over her head and toss it to the side, she rolls her hips. I groan, feeling her core rub against my hardening cock. There are only a few thin layers separating us as I get up and carry her inside the house.

Hadley groans as I push her up against a wall. Her legs wrap around my waist as her fingers sink into my hair. I groan and push my hips forward. Hadley digs her ankles into my back.

"I love you," Hadley says as I flick the clasp on her bra open and let it fall to the ground. "Fuck, I love you."

"I love you too. So fucking much." My voice is raspy as I dip my head.

Her back arches as my fingers dig into the flesh at her ass. My tongue flicks over her nipple before I take the sensitive bud into my mouth. I groan as her hands leave my hair, digging into my shoulders as I tease her nipple into a hard peak before switching to the other.

"I need you," she says, gasping as I pull us away from the wall.

My cock throbs with every brush against her core as I walk down the hall with her in my arms. I step into my office and shove the papers to the floor before setting her down on my desk.

Hadley slides off the desk and kneels in front of me. Her tongue darts out to lick her lips as she pulls down my shorts and boxers. All I can think about are those full lips wrapped around my cock.

"You look gorgeous down on your knees for me."

She smirks and wraps her hand around my cock. Her thumb drifts over the head, swirling around the droplet at the tip. Hadley strokes me soft and slow, teasing as her tongue slides over the tip.

"Stop teasing me and take my cock in your pretty little mouth. I want to feel you taking me deep."

My fingers sink into her hair and I pull it back from her face. She moans as I brush the tip of my cock against her lips. On the second pass, she opens her mouth, hollows her cheeks, and sucks me deep.

I moan, using my grip on her hair to set the pace. Her fingers dig into my thighs as she grazes her teeth over my length.

"Fuck." I watch my cock sliding between her lips, "I want you to sit on the edge of my desk and spread your legs."

Lust flashes through her eyes as she moves faster, her head bobbing as she sucks me harder. My cock throbs in her mouth as I hold back. I don't want to finish with her yet. I want to enjoy the feeling of being with the woman I love for as long as possible.

"Get up and get your ass on my desk or I'll do it for you."

Hadley gets to her feet and grins, stripping out of the last of her clothing before sitting on the edge of the desk. I groan as she leans back and braces herself with one hand before spreading her legs.

Her fingers trail down her neck and between her breasts. I grip my cock as she teases herself, rolling one nipple and then the other. When I look down at her pussy, it is dripping wet as she swirls her fingers around her clit.

When she sinks her fingers into her pussy, my control snaps.

I close the distance between us and take her hand,

guiding it faster until she is moaning and her head rolls back on her shoulders.

Just before she comes, I pull her hand away from her core to lick her fingers clean. She watches me with hooded eyes as my tongue flicks between her fingers.

As soon as I'm done tasting her, I get to my knees between her legs. Hadley arches her back as I run my hands up and down her inner thighs. She's teetering on the edge of an orgasm and all I want to do is tease her until she falls off that edge.

I hook one of her legs over my shoulder before licking her wet slit, groaning at the taste of her on my tongue. Hadley writhes against my face as I slide my fingers into her core while teasing her clit with my tongue.

Hadley moans as her fingers weave through my hair. She holds my face against her as her inner walls pulsate around my fingers. I move my fingers faster, my tongue flattening against her clit as she comes.

"Good girl," I say as I pepper kisses up and down her inner thighs.

"I need you," she says, her voice breathy as she looks at me with fire in her eyes. "I need you now. Please."

"What do you want me to do to you?" I ask as I stand and press my thumb against her clit, moving it in a lazy circle. "Do you want to come again?"

"Yes. Please." Hadley hooks a leg around my hip and pulls me to her. "I want to feel your cock buried in me."

I grab her hips and enter her in a quick thrust. Hadley's fingers dig into my shoulders as she rolls her hips. I pull out and slam back into her, burying myself to the hilt.

Her pussy pulses around me as her back arches. I kiss her soft and slow, my thrusts lazy and long. I take my time to run my hands over every inch of her body, trying to commit her to memory.

"I love you," she says, breathless as I slide a hand between us and toy with her clit.

"I love you so much." I nip at her bottom lip before I start rocking my hips faster.

Hadley moans as I hook my arm under her thigh and pull her leg higher, allowing me to drive myself deeper into her. Her fingers claw at my shoulders, her nails raking my skin as my cock throbs.

Her pussy clenches around me as her orgasm takes over her. She clings to me as I thrust harder and faster, needing more of her. I keep thrusting until my cock stiffens. It only takes the feeling of her pussy squeezing me to send me over the edge. My orgasm comes hard and fast as I still and keep myself deep inside her.

"It's a good thing I can't get pregnant again," she says, her tone teasing as I pull out of her.

Her cheeks are a rosy red and her smile stretches from one side of her face to the other. Her hair is a tangled mess and her makeup is slightly smudged from our long day, but I don't think she's ever been more beautiful.

"Race you to the bedroom," Hadley says as she slides off the desk. "Last one there has to make the other breakfast in bed."

I grin and watch her take off running, giving her a head-start before I follow after her.

As I catch her and pin her against the wall, I can't believe that she is the woman I am lucky enough to spend my life with.

23

HADLEY

For the last few days, I've been walking on clouds even though I've been exhausted. Between the pregnancy and getting things ready for the baby, I run out of energy in the early afternoon.

Combine that with learning to fight safely while pregnant and working on my shooting, and I drop into bed exhausted shortly after dinner.

When I wake up in the morning, we do it all over again.

I wouldn't change it for the world, though. Every moment I get to spend with Jovan is another one where I see the life I want developing in front of me. He is everything that I've ever wanted, even if how our relationship started wasn't the most ideal situation.

That's why when I wake up in the middle of the night, I roll closer to him. Jovan yawns and shuffles closer to me, wrapping his arm around my waist. Pale moonlight streams through the window in front of me, illuminating a path in the middle of the room.

"Well, isn't this cute?" a deep voice says.

I roll onto my back to see a man standing on the other

side of the bed. He has a gun in his hand and a black mask pulled over his face.

"Jovan," I say, shaking his shoulder. "Wake up."

He groans but his eyes open. When they do, he rolls over and sees the man. No sooner does he see the man, then he is on his feet.

I scramble to my side of the bed and rip open my nightstand drawer as the heavy thud of fists sounds from behind me. My hands are shaking as I open the little safe in the drawer and pull out my gun. I make sure that it is loaded as I turn and look at the men who are still fighting.

There is no clear shot.

"Who are you and what are you doing here?" Jovan asks as the man shoves him against a wall.

"Fuck you," the man says. "It doesn't matter who I am. All you need to know is that you're going to die tonight."

My mind is racing as I aim the gun at the man. Jovan lunges forward and catches the man around the waist, slamming him into the ground. He scrambles to get on top of the masked man, throwing punch after punch.

The man throws Jovan off and is on top of him in an instant. My heart skips a beat but this is my chance. I try to will the shaking out of my hands. I can't risk missing and hitting Jovan.

You need to take the shot.

I don't want to kill him.

It's then that the man pulls out a long knife. He advances on Jovan as Jovan grabs the lamp from the nightstand and smashes him over the head with it. As soon as the man is disoriented, Jovan drops his shoulder and tackles the man into the floor. His face twists up in pain as he tries to stay on top of the man.

The man flips them over, his mask falling off in the process. Carlos grins down at Jovan, raising the knife high above his head.

I have to do it. *Now.*

As my finger squeezes the trigger, I don't think about the fact that I'm going to kill a man. Instead, I think about the life of the person I'm saving. The man I love. The father of my child.

Carlos shouts, the knife clattering to the floor as the bullet connects with his shoulder.

I know what kind of man Carlos is. A bullet to the shoulder isn't going to stop him for long. He wraps a hand around Jovan's neck and squeezes as I take aim again.

The bullet hits Carlos in the side of the head. Jovan pushes Carlos off as blood cascades down the side of his face. I stare at the body slumped on the floor and the crimson blood staining the hardwood.

My chest starts to constrict as I look between the gun and Carlos. While I might not have been a fan of the man, I didn't want to be the one to kill him. In a perfect world, this would have been someone else's problem. I wouldn't have shot a man dead.

This is what I get for getting wrapped up in the cartel.

Felix Domingos wants Jovan dead. He has no reason to bother with me. I shouldn't be here. I need to protect my baby.

Although, I know that isn't true. Felix has some sort of interest in me, though I'm not sure what. He wants me dead because I'm connected to Jovan. But maybe it has something to do with my parents too.

Stop thinking about it. You're not doing yourself any favors by getting more entrenched in the cartel.

I take a deep breath as Jovan stands in front of me. He gently takes the gun from my hands and disassembles it. After he sets the gun down on the bed, he looks at me, his gaze flickering around my face like he's searching for something.

"Hadley, are you alright? Did you get hurt at all?"

"There is a dead man in our bedroom." I look at Carlos's body and shake my head. My vision starts to blur as I continue to stare at him. "There is a dead body in our room and I'm the one who killed him. I killed a man. How could I do that, Jovan?"

"Listen, you did what you had to." Jovan tries to take my hands in his but I pull them back. "Carlos was going to kill me. He might have killed you and the baby after. You did what you had to. You kept us safe."

"No." I take a step back and stare at what I've done. "No. I killed a man. Our child was put in even more danger. Carlos was able to get in our house. He was able to stand over our bed and wake us up. Where the hell is everyone else?"

"That's what I'm going to find out," Jovan says as he puts the gun on the bed back together and tucks it in his waistband. "I want you to stay here until I get back."

"No." I head for the closet and take a suitcase down from the top shelf. "I need to leave, Jovan. Our baby almost died tonight. I'm not going to sit around and wait for that to happen again. Not when I can do something to stop it."

"Hadley," he says, his voice low. "I have to go clear the rest of the house. I'll be back in a minute and then we're going to talk about this."

I don't say anything. As much as I want to be with him,

my mind is made up on the matter. I'm not going to continue to put our baby in the path of danger when I can do something to protect them.

I have to make sure the baby is safe and that is the only thing that matters. If that means that I have to give up the man I love, then that is what I'm going to do.

It's going to gut me every single day, but I care about our baby and keeping them protected more than I care about my love life.

We might find our way back to each other eventually, but right now, this is what needs to happen.

"Alright, the house is clear. I have men unconscious outside but none of them are dead. Alessio is on his way with more men and then we are going to get this mess cleaned up," Jovan says as he walks back into the room.

I pull open drawers and pull out clothing, tossing them into the open suitcase on the floor. As I pack, I try my hardest to hold back tears. I'm not going to cry over this. I'm going to make sure that we both walk away feeling as good as we can about the situation.

"Hadley, what are you doing?" Jovan asks, his voice broken as he appears in the doorway to the closet. "I told you that I was going to take care of everything. You don't have to leave."

I shake my head and bite my lip. "Jovan, you said that you weren't going to hold me back if I needed to go. I want you to know that this isn't because I don't love you. I do, so much, and you are doing a fantastic job protecting us. I just need some space."

He sighs and his eyes shine as he looks at me. "This was one bad night, Hadley. Not every night is going to be like this. If you stay, we can get everything figured out. I promise we can. I'll kill Felix tomorrow, if that's what it takes."

"It doesn't matter if you kill him tomorrow when you don't know how deep the disloyalty runs." I give him a sad smile as I shove another armful of clothing into the suitcase. "We both know that you still have a lot of digging to do. It's going to be easier with me out of the way."

"Is that really what you think?" He steps into the closet, his arms hovering at his sides like he doesn't know what to do with them. "Do you really think that I can focus while you're off running around somewhere?"

"It's not going to be somewhere. I sent Kennedy a message. I'm going to be staying with her and Rio. You can send whoever else you want to watch over me too. I don't want to make this any harder than it needs to be, Jovan."

He nods even though it looks like it kills him. "So, that's it, then. You're abandoning your family for your own needs. Just like your parents. You keep people at a distance so they can't hurt you. The entire time we've been together, you've been looking for a reason to run away."

"That's not true!"

"It *is* true. I should have known when I found out that you were the one who set fire to your childhood home." Jovan scoffs and steps out of the closet, crossing his arms. "You really are just like your parents. They would have done anything to erase their past as well. Hell, they didn't give a shit if they had a future. You don't seem to either."

It feels like all the air has been knocked from my lungs.

Breathing feels like it is impossible as I kneel on the ground to zip up the suitcase.

Even though I know he is just saying those things because he's hurt, it still cuts deep.

"How did you find out about my family home?" I ask, my voice wavering slightly. "Nobody was supposed to know about that."

"You've burned every bridge you ever built, Hadley. Did you really think that Carlos was going to keep your little secret after everything that you've said to him over the years?"

My vision blurs as I look at Jovan. "I don't know who you are, but I want you to know that I still love you. The baby is still going to be a part of your life and I hope that someday I can be too."

His eyes narrow. "Go, Hadley. I told you that I wouldn't stop you if you thought that it was for the best."

"I'll talk to you in a few days."

I pick up my suitcase and head for the front door. With each step, I feel like I'm making the biggest mistake of my life but I can't turn back now. I've said what I needed to say and I made the decision to leave.

The only thing that makes me strong enough to keep one foot moving in front of the other is the knowledge that once it's safe again, I'll come back to him.

Although, I don't know how I can be with him if he is going to throw my parents in my face when we disagree. Though I love him, there are some things I can't overlook.

But is there really a way to be with him when we are both so damaged? When we both have ghosts that haunt us day in and day out?

24

JOVAN

I'm sorry I'm such an asshole.

I never should have thrown your parents in your face like that.

I should have told you the moment I found out you started the fire.

I'm sorry. I'm so fucking sorry.

Out of the million things I could say to Hadley about what happened between us last night, those are the thoughts that keep circling around. I need to apologize to her. I need to make things right between us, even though it will still mean having her out of my life for a little while.

I had told her that I wasn't going to stop her and then I made it hell on her to leave.

I should have been supportive. I could have helped her pack and then brought her over to Kennedy's. Hell, I should have told her that I would be waiting for her whenever she was ready to talk about what would come next for us.

Instead, I did everything wrong and I have only myself to blame for the way I reacted.

I'm an asshole.

As I stand outside Kennedy's apartment building and look up at the window I know is hers, I wonder if Hadley is awake yet. If she is even going to be willing to talk to me after the night we had last night.

If I was her, I don't know that I would be too willing to talk to me. Hell, I would probably tell me to get lost.

Hadley isn't like that, though. She loves me as much as I love her. She isn't going anywhere, she is just doing what she feels she needs to for our baby.

Even though it hurts, I love her even more for that.

She is stronger than I am. She was the one who walked away when she knew it was getting dangerous.

The fact that it was days after I told her that I love her stung, but I understand why.

I can't have men coming into my bedroom and trying to kill me while I sleep. The people guarding my home need to do a better job. I have other cartel members training to be on protection detail, but I don't think that will be enough to get Hadley to come home.

"So," Kennedy says as she appears at my side. "Do you want me to walk up there with you?"

"I thought you were in there with her. Is Rio up there?"

Kennedy shakes her head. "No. Hadley said that you were sending someone after her to watch over her. She arrived when I was getting home from work so we went to bed. I went to the gym this morning. I thought I saw one of your men sitting outside watching the apartment."

My blood runs cold. I didn't send anyone after her last night. I thought that Rio would be here to take care of her and there would be no point in sending anyone else.

"Where is Rio?"

Kennedy digs through her purse, her eyes wide as if she is thinking the same thing I am. I don't know how much Rio tells her, but I know she hears enough in the club. She would have a vague idea of what is going on with Felix.

"He sent you a message last night. Somebody bailed on an arms run. He isn't going to be back until tomorrow."

I pull out my phone and check it. I thought that the last message would have been about the training we needed to do with the soldiers, but instead, it was one from Rio. Sure enough, he was going on the biggest arms run we had done this year.

"I'm going up there," I say as Kennedy hands me her keys. "Rio only left a few hours ago. I'm sending a helicopter to pick him up. I need his ass back here."

"I'll call him."

"Good," I say as I pull out my car keys and hand them to her. "I want you to go sit in the car with the doors locked. It's armored. Nobody will be able to try anything. Stay in there and don't come out for anyone other than me, got it?"

Kennedy nods, a determined look on her face. "Do you think anything happened?"

My stomach lurches and bile rises in my throat. "I don't know."

"I never should have left her. I'm sorry." Kennedy's eyes shine with unshed tears. She pulls her phone out of her purse and starts walking to the car.

For a moment, I can see what Rio sees in her. She loves people fiercely, but she also seems like the kind of woman you would want by your side in an emergency. She is steady and strong in a way that not many people are when lives are on the line.

I send a quick message to my helicopter pilot and another one to Rio before taking the first step toward the building. I know what I'm going to find in there, but I hope I'm wrong.

I head into the building, taking the stairs two at a time to get to Kennedy's floor. My heart is trying to break through my ribcage as I run down the hall and unlock the door.

The apartment is dark when I walk inside but all it takes is flicking on the lights to see blood on the floor. I pull out my gun and start walking slowly through the rooms, looking for anywhere anyone might be hiding.

When I finish clearing the apartment, I look back down at the blood stains on the ground. There are no long streaks, so she left walking.

It's a small comfort, but it's one that I'll take right now. I don't know what's happened to her but I know it was Felix.

I follow the blood trail to where it divides in front of the fridge.

Good. Looks like Hadley put up a fight.

The thought is enough to make me swell with pride as I look at the pictures on the fridge for anything that doesn't belong. Felix is the kind of man who likes to play games. Leaving the answer to where he took Hadley would be part of his game.

After looking through all the pictures, I finally find one hidden behind a grocery list. The picture has a bloody fingerprint on the corner and in the center is a boat at one of the local marinas.

"Fuck," I say, taking the picture off the fridge and folding it to fit in my pocket.

The last thing I want to do is meet him out on the water. There are too many unknowns about what he could do. There is no escape if he decides to ambush us.

I'm fucked.

As I leave the apartment, I hope the helicopter brings Rio back fast. I'm going to need him if I hope to get this done.

At least Alessio is in town too.

I pull out my phone and call him, listening to the rings and feeling more and more like the worst is happening to Hadley.

"Hey," Alessio says. "We've just finished looking through some of the buildings Felix's family used to own. No sign of him there."

"No. There wouldn't be," I say, my voice sounding choked. "He's got Hadley, Alessio. He took her and I have to go get her back."

"Whatever you need, Jovan," Alessio says as I hear something shuffling in the background. "I'm getting into my car now. Where is he taking her?"

"The marina. I can't go there. He's waiting for me."

Alessio chuckles. "Don't you worry. I'll get there and we'll keep an eye out for her."

"Don't move until I send you a message later with the plan. Just keep an eye on him for now." My heart is hammering in my chest as I get in my car. I need to make sure that nothing is going to happen to Hadley. I can't risk anyone getting too close before Felix is ready.

"Don't worry, Jovan. We're going to make sure that she is safe and everything is alright with her. He isn't going to do anything to her. I promise."

I swallow the lump in my throat. "Don't make promises you can't keep, Alessio."

"Nothing is going to happen to her."

"I hope you're right," I say before thanking him, ending the call, and starting the engine.

Please let Alessio be right. I don't know how to keep going on in life if anything happens to Hadley or our baby.

"Sorry I took so long, boss," Rio says, two hours later when he meets me in my kitchen. "Why are we meeting here and not going straight to the marina? Isn't that where Felix has her?"

"He does but he has a meeting time set for us. He said that if he saw us before then, he would kill her without a second thought. I'm not willing to take the risk when Hadley's life is hanging in the balance."

Rio nods and takes a seat at my kitchen island. "Alright, so how are we going to do this? There is no way to sneak up on him in the water if he decides to lead us out there. We're going to have to pull alongside him and get on."

There is no doubt in my mind that Felix is going to lead us out in the water. It's what makes the most sense. Getting us out where nobody can see what is going to happen is the only way to keep the coast guard from arriving before the job is done.

I'm going to kill that fucker for what he's done to my family.

I sigh as I look at Rio. "Though he says he wants to meet in the marina, you know as well as I do that he is going to want as few witnesses as possible."

"What do you want to do when that happens?" Rio drums his fingers on the counter. "There won't be any way to avoid going out to him if that's what he's going to do."

"I don't want to tie our boat to his. If we do that, then we're going to lose our only method of escape short of commandeering his boat. We won't know what kind of traps he has rigged and where. We could risk setting something off that could kill all of us if we take his boat. I don't want to do that. We're going to destroy that boat and everyone on it, which means that we need ours as the getaway."

"What do you want to do, then?"

I open the fridge and grab a bottle of water, taking a long sip. "You're going to get me as close to the boat as you can. I'll swim the rest of the way. After that, I want you to take the boat out until I give you my signal."

"Jovan, this is a fucking death wish. You can't go onto that boat alone."

"Well, we don't have much of an option here. I can't trust anybody other than you and Alessio right now, and he is keeping an eye on her, so you're going to have to take me, which means I have to board his boat alone because we need a getaway driver, AKA you." I run my hand down my face and slump back against the counter. "I wish that there was another way to handle it, but Felix is forcing us into the game he wants to play."

"I'm getting off the boat and coming with you." Rio glares at me. "You might be the boss, but you're also my best friend. You took care of Kennedy for me and got her to safety, I'm going to do the same for you."

"You know that neither of us may get off that boat," I say before taking another sip of water. "We're walking into a death trap and there's not much either of us is going to be able to do about it."

"When do we meet with Felix?"

"Twelve hours from now. Kennedy is in one of my spare rooms. I suggest you spend all the time with her that you can before we leave."

Rio gives me a sad smile and gets up from his seat. "Thank you. I'll be ready to go when you are. For what it's worth, I feel horrible that I wasn't there last night and this morning. If I had been, this might not have happened."

I shake my head and swallow the lump in my throat. "This would have happened one way or another. Right now,

I can be certain that Hadley is alive. If anyone else had been there with her, she might not be."

Though Rio gives a sharp nod before turning away, I still see the guilt written all over his face.

However, that guilt is only half of what I feel because this is all my fault. I might lose Hadley and the baby.

And I have nobody to blame but myself.

When I see Hadley again, I'm going to apologize for everything I said and didn't say last night. I'm going to make sure she knows how much I love her and our child. I want her to know everything.

I don't want to die with any regrets.

I'm going to spend the next few hours getting ready for every outcome. I need to make sure that the car is loaded with weapons and medical supplies. The doctor is already on standby and going to be at the marina when we get there.

Even if I don't get off the boat, I'm going to make damn sure Hadley does.

Walking onto that boat is going to be like signing my life away. I know that. Felix is going to do everything in his power to make sure that one of us dies today. This is the game he has been playing since he came back to Miami. It was all coming to this moment.

He either kills me, or I kill him.

I'm not going to let it be me.

Not when I have my family to live for.

25

HADLEY

I'VE BEEN TRAPPED IN A LITTLE ROOM ON A BOAT FOR what feels like the better part of the day.

Though the scent of the salt water calms me, it isn't enough to shake the fear that I'm going to die today.

Ever since Felix walked into Kennedy's apartment early this morning, I knew I was going to die, it was only a matter of when.

Since then, I've been trying to think of everything that I can do to stay alive. So far, Felix and his men have left me to my own devices. There's not much I can do in the room they've locked me in.

For the last couple of hours, I've been looking around for something that might help me but there is nothing. No guns or knives hidden in any of the secret compartments I've found. Not even a pen I could stab them through the eye with.

I'm screwed if I don't find something to use as a weapon.

Sooner or later, Felix is going to come for me and he's going to kill me. I have to be ready to kill him first.

The thought makes me sick to my stomach. I don't want

to kill any more people. That was why I left Jovan's home in the first place. I was supposed to be able to put a little distance between us.

It had been only a couple hours from the time I left him to the time I was attacked and kidnapped.

I should have known that Felix had people watching me. I should have known that they were going to come for me the moment that I was alone.

I was stupid. I thought that I was going to be safe.

After all these years, I know better than to leave myself vulnerable but I did it anyway.

I'm even more sorry because I won't be able to tell Jovan how much I regret leaving him. That I won't tell him once again how much I love him.

I pace around the room, looking for anything that I might be able to use. All of the knobs and handles are securely bolted in. There are no rogue pairs of scissors or tweezers left in the drawers.

Felix and his men thought of everything they needed to remove before locking me in here. I sigh and run my hands through my hair, wincing when my fingers brush against the bump on my head.

Fucking idiot.

Getting hit over the head had been my own stupid fault. I had turned my back on Felix long enough to try and reach for the gun Kennedy kept hidden in her nightstand and he had taken the opportunity to bring a lamp down on me.

It *had* been mildly ironic to me at the time but now I'm just pissed off.

There has to be something here that I can use.

I get on my hands and knees, crawling along the floor. I check the base of the cabinets for any loose piece of wood before making my way over to the bed frame.

As I run my hands along the metal bed frame, I look for anything that might be loose enough to pull off. When my hand finally catches on a piece of metal, hope starts to soar within me.

I'm not going down without a fucking fight.

I get up and head to the door, pressing my ear against the wood and listening for a few minutes. When I don't hear anyone nearby, I go back to the bed and start pulling on the piece of metal.

Though I get a shallow cut on my hand from the sharp edge, I manage to pull off a piece that is nearly a foot long. One of the ends has a nice point to it and another side is fairly sharp.

It's not much, but it will be enough to protect myself.

———

"Alright, honey," Felix says as he walks into the room with a man at his side. "It's showtime. Your little boyfriend should be here soon and then we are all going to play a game. It's going to be a fun game, I think. Although, maybe if you're nice, I might let you live. You could be useful to me."

"Go to hell," I say as I sit on the edge of the bed.

Beneath the sheet I have draped over my lap, I hold the piece of metal. Felix looks at me, his beady eyes traveling my body, but he doesn't linger on my lap.

"Honey," Felix says, his tone patronizing as the other man stalks over to me. "I've been to hell and back. However, you're going to find out what happens to people who disrespect me. Jovan may be willing to put up with it, but I'm not."

As the man lunges for me, I stand up with my piece of

metal. He shouts as I drive the metal upward, into his torso. His hands clasp his torso as blood begins to pour through his fingers.

I pull the piece of metal out as the man stumbles toward the bed. As I drive the metal through his neck, my heart races. I feel like I'm going to throw up but I do my best to keep the rising bile down.

Felix claps as the man's blood spills across the bed. "Very good, Hadley. I wasn't sure that you had it in you. Of course, you are your parents' daughter. Your mother would have done the same thing if I didn't make sure she was kept too high to turn on me."

My stomach plummets as I face Felix, the blood-covered weapon in my hand. Based on the look on his face, I'm not going to be able to attack him the same way I did to his man. I don't have the element of surprise on my side any longer.

"Come now, Hadley. You had to know that your parents were connected to the Domingos cartel. I used to come and go from your home all the time when you were a little girl. When I was hiding out there, we used to play with your dolls. You would make up the wildest stories."

Even though I don't want to believe him — and I don't remember anything about him being in my home — a little voice in the back of my mind says that he's telling the truth.

It wouldn't be the first time I repressed my memories.

"Losing your parents is one of my biggest regrets," Felix says, grinning as he leans against one of the cabinets and crosses his arms.

"I don't know what you're talking about. I don't remember any of that."

Felix shrugs. "You wouldn't, would you? There was so much going on in your life at that time. It's no wonder that things have fallen through the cracks. Although, I have to admit that I was rather impressed when you set that fire. It got me thinking about what I would do when I returned to Miami for good."

"I still don't know what you're talking about." I tighten my grip on the piece of metal. "Let me go. I promise to leave before Jovan gets here. I can make sure that he doesn't come after you."

He smirks and shakes his head. "I'm afraid that this has been a long time coming. You have your parents to thank for my being back, though. They worked as informants against the Ruiz cartel. And then after Jovan slaughtered my family, I had them turn their attention to his cartel."

"Ruiz, as in Carlos?"

"Now you're starting to put it together. Awful shame that you murdered him. Although, his brother is probably glad. It leaves him without another mess to clean up."

My head is spinning with the new information. Though I wish that I could say I'm surprised to find out that my parents are informants, I'm not. They would do anything for drugs. If that meant spying on one cartel and feeding information to another, then that is what they would do.

"Now," Felix says as he stands up straight. "You can either put that down and come with me, or I can drag you out of here. Either way, we have to be on the deck soon for our meeting with your boyfriend."

"He's not going to get himself trapped on this boat with you," I say, though I know if there's one thing I can count on when it comes to Jovan, it's that he will do anything he can to protect his family.

Felix laughs and shakes his head as he takes slow steps toward me. "You and I both know that isn't true." And damn if he isn't right.

My heart is racing and my stomach tosses and turns. I feel like I'm going to be sick but I have to do whatever I can to hold it together. I have to be in control. One wrong move on my end could get the baby killed before Jovan even gets here.

I put my hand on my stomach. *Everything is going to be okay, little one. We're going to make it out of this just fine.*

At least, I hope so.

"Put the metal down and come with me, Hadley. I don't want to make this any harder than it needs to be."

I put the piece of metal down as he closes the distance between us. I don't want to end up dead, and I know he won't hesitate to kill me if I try something funny.

Although, if he does that, he loses whatever power he has over Jovan. If I can just stall him long enough, maybe Jovan can get on the boat before Felix and his men even know he's here.

Felix's guard is down as he stands in front of me. He grabs my chin and tilts my face up, smirking when I scowl.

"You got your mother's beauty. At least, what she had before she took all those drugs. It's a shame that Carlos got her hooked in the first place. Your father, well, there would have been no saving him. Your mother on the other hand, she always wanted to quit. Kept trying to get clean for you."

His words hurt worse than any stab wound ever could. I never knew that my mom was trying to get clean for me. She never talked about it.

"After I'm done with you, I'm going to have to go deal with that fool, Alessio Marchetti. He was supposed to kill the both of you long before I ever did. That's why I sent word of your parents being alive around town. Of you helping hide them. So that he'd do something about you to protect his friend and then Jovan would go after him demanding retribution, and he'd die a pitiful death at the hands of his friend too."

"That was you?"

His smile is predatory as he nods. "Brilliant, right? If Alessio wasn't such an incompetent, useless asshole."

"Alessio isn't incompetent. He's smarter than you give him credit for and a true friend. He wouldn't betray Jovan like that. And speaking of, Jovan isn't going to let you off this boat and we both know it," I say, tearing away from him.

I reach down and grab the piece of metal from the bed, swinging it straight into Felix's crotch. He groans and drops to the ground as I take off running for the door with the metal still in my hand.

All I need to do is get off the boat.

I'm heading up the stairs when a hand grabs my hair and pulls me back down. I scream as I hit the floor, pain radiating through my body.

"You are a clever little bitch, aren't you?" Felix growls beside my ear. "It really is too bad that I'm going to have to kill you. I was going to leave you and your baby alive. Of course, you would have been working for me for the rest of your life, but I would have thought that was better than death."

"Fuck you," I say, spitting the blood that pools in my mouth at him. "You're going to die for what you've done to me."

"I haven't done anything yet." He lets go of my hair and grabs my bicep, hauling me to my feet. "In fact, I'm just getting started. For a while, I thought it was going to be only you I got to kill. Imagine my surprise when I broke into your apartment and found those ultrasound pictures."

'You touch my baby and I will kill you myself," I say, my

hands curling into fists. I try to pull my arm free but he only tightens his grip as he drags me through the boat.

"Hadley, I've already told you that I don't want to make this any harder than it has to be. If you would stop fighting me every step of the way, then it might not be so bad."

"Says the man who wants to kill my family."

Felix laughs as we reach the top deck. He shoves me onto one of the couches and nods at a man standing nearby. The man moves closer to me, his gaze weary and his hand on his gun.

I wonder if he knows what I did to his buddy.

As I smile at him, he looks away.

"She's a little girl," Felix says, rolling his eyes. "You act as if she's something to be feared."

"I'm not." I smile brightly at the man before glancing over Felix's shoulder. "But he is."

Jovan raises his gun as he stands on the deck dripping wet. A shot rings out and the man standing beside me falls to the ground.

"Get his gun, Hadley," Jovan says as Felix pulls his own weapon.

"Not so fast," Felix says, pointing his gun at me. "Our little game is just getting started."

26

JOVAN

Hadley looks at me with wide eyes. Her gaze darts to the dead man and the gun on the ground. I give a small shake of my head as Felix heads toward her. He keeps his gun trained on her, making sure that I can't kill him without potentially killing my family too.

Gunshots ring out from the deck below us. Alessio, Rio and I landed on the boat at the same time, but I had heard Hadley cussing Felix out as he brought her to the top deck.

My little spitfire. Still won't let anybody push her around, even when she could die.

"Now," Felix says as he looks between the two of us. "This is how this game is going to go. I'm going to kill your family and then I'm going to kill you. It won't be quick, though. No, you deserve to suffer for all that you've done."

"Take me," I say as he pulls Hadley to her feet and presses the gun against her head. "Let Hadley go and take me. She doesn't need to be a part of this. She didn't do anything wrong."

Hadley smirks, though I can see the tears shining in her eyes. "Well, I did hit him in the dick with some metal.

Killed a guy too. So, I think that saying I did nothing wrong would be a bit of a stretch."

"Now is not the time to be a smartass," I say, though I'm proud of her. I knew that she wouldn't make it easy on Felix and I'm happy to see that she hasn't. He doesn't deserve easy.

Felix tightens his hold on her and rams the gun into her temple. She winces in pain before turning to scowl at him. Seeing the gun pressed between her eyebrows makes me feel sick. In a moment's notice, I could lose her and our child.

"Hadley, I love you, but I need you to let me handle this," I say, my tone soft as Felix moves to stand behind Hadley. "I'm going to get us out of this but I need you to stop egging him on."

She glances at me from the corner of her eye. The first tear starts to roll down her cheeks as she nods. My heart breaks seeing the way she cradles her stomach, as if her hands are going to be enough to protect our baby.

"Why don't we talk about this like men?" I put my gun down, though I know it is a risky move.

However, it's calculated. Felix wants to take his time with me. He wants to make sure that I truly suffer.

That isn't going to happen if he can't get close to me. He knows that the minute Hadley is no longer in my line of fire, I will kill him.

The only way to play his game is to make myself defenseless and hope that Rio or Alessio get up here in time to save Hadley.

"You really think that I'm stupid enough to come near you? Throw the gun overboard," Felix says, jerking his chin toward the side of the boat.

I do as he says, picking up the gun and throwing it hard

over the side. When I turn back to him, I lift my shirt and spin in a slow circle. I have nothing else on me. No guns. No knives.

"Hadley, go sit over there." Felix points the gun in the direction of the bar. "Make me a drink to enjoy while I rip your boyfriend's teeth out of his head. After that, I think I might want something else for ripping his nails out."

"Fucking try it," I say, standing with my arms wide open. "You want me, here I am."

More gunshots echo through the evening as the waves lap against the sides of the boat. It would be a beautiful night if I wasn't taunting a man to kill me.

"Hadley," I say as she walks toward the bar. "I love you. And our baby. I'm so sorry for dragging you into this mess and I want you to know that I'm going to do whatever it takes to get you out of it."

"I love you too," she says, her breath hitching as she steps behind the bar. "We're going to be okay."

Felix clears his throat as he saunters toward me. "If the two of you are done, I have business to attend to."

As he walks toward me, Hadley watches him. I glance away from her, keeping my attention on Felix. He tucks his gun into the holster at his hip and pulls a knife out of his pocket.

"Seems kind of unfair that I don't have a weapon, don't you think?" I ask, taunting him as I start walking backward. "What are people going to say about you? Sure, you took me down but I didn't have a chance to fight back against it."

"You really think that I'm going to fall for that shit?"

I shrug and take another few steps back before circling and moving until I stand between Felix and Hadley. As soon as I'm dead, I know he's going to go after her. I have to stall for enough time until one of my guys can get up here.

Felix grins as he shifts the knife from one hand to the other and back again. "There is no way for you out of this. You can stop playing whatever game you're playing. I'm going to kill you and then I'm going to kill your girlfriend."

"Jovan!" Alessio shouts.

I glance at the direction his voice comes from in time to catch a gun. At the same time, Felix shouts. I turn and face him in time to see Hadley punch him in the face, her foot on his wrist to keep herself from getting stabbed.

It looks like all of her self-defense lessons are paying off.

"You fucking bitch," Felix says, his voice a growl before he spits blood to the side.

I run over to them with the gun pointed at Felix's head. Hadley puts pressure on his wrist until he drops the knife. She picks up the knife and steps away, hurrying over to where Rio is now standing with Alessio.

"Take her to our boat," I say without looking at them.

Alessio raises his gun and aims it at Felix. Though he has a clear shot too, we both know that I have to be the one to kill Felix.

I need to be the one to kill Felix for everything he has done to our family.

"Like hell," Hadley says, venom in her voice. "I want to see the bastard die."

Felix gets to his feet. "You don't have the balls."

"This is for fucking with my family." Gun trained on the spot between his eyebrows, I pull the trigger as he goes for the gun at his hip.

Felix falls to the ground, blood streaming down his face. I shoot him again for good measure. Hadley comes over and kicks his body in the ribs. "Serves you right, fucker."

When I turn to Hadley, tears are shining in her eyes and her hands are shaking as they hold the knife.

"It's okay," I say as I disassemble the gun and toss the pieces overboard. I walk over to Hadley and pull her into my arms. "Everything is going to be okay. We're going to go home and everything is going to be fine. You're safe now. Our baby is safe now."

Her arms circle my waist and she holds me tight. I kiss the top of her head and hug her until she pulls away and nods. "Everything is going to be okay."

"We're going to take you back to the boat and then we are going to burn this one. After that, I'm going to take you home and we're going to spend the rest of the night relaxing."

I hold her hand as we head down to the lower deck. Rio jumps in the small tender and speeds across the water to our boat before bringing it closer. Alessio and I help Hadley from one boat and to the other.

As soon as she is on my boat, she tosses the knife into the ocean and rubs her hands on her pants.

"I need you to stay right here," I say, cupping her face as I lean between the two boats. I kiss her quickly before pulling away. "I love you and everything is going to be alright. I'll be back in a minute."

Even though the last thing I want to do is walk away from her, I have a crime scene to dispose of.

Relief fills me at the thought of this finally being over. I don't have to deal with Felix anymore. He can no longer threaten my family. This was enough to show me there are traitors among our ranks and they are going down with their leader. The clean-up has already started before I left home earlier and by this time tomorrow, all of the bad apples will be in the trash where they belong,

The cartel will be stronger and tighter when all is said and done.

For now, I'm thankful that we're alive and safe and our baby is going to be here soon.

We're going to move forward together without anyone threatening to hold us back.

THE SHOWER STEAM CLOUDS THE GLASS WALLS AS I take my time washing the blood from Hadley's hair. The cuts on her body are small, but they're there. Rage fills me when I think about how Felix attacked her and kidnapped her.

"I love you," I say as I kiss her shoulder, avoiding a cut near her neck. "I'm sorry that you had to go through that. I thought that Rio would be there to protect you. I didn't know he wasn't there."

Hadley smiles and runs her hands down my torso. "Jovan, it's fine. We're okay now. Felix would have come after me one way or another. There is no way you would have been able to protect me every hour of every day."

I frown and she reaches up to smooth away the lines at the corner of my mouth. "How are you feeling?"

"I love you." Hadley kisses the corner of my mouth. "I don't feel great right now. The doctor said that the baby was fine when he checked over me. It's just everything else that is making me feel like shit. It's been a long day."

I pull her into a tight embrace. "I'm sorry about what I said yesterday. You are nothing like your parents. I lashed out because I was scared of losing you, even after promising that you could walk away if you needed to. The thought of losing you almost destroyed me."

"It's okay," she says softly as she kisses my collarbone. "We're okay now. We're going to work to be the best that we can be for each other and neither of us is going to lose our family ever again."

The water starts to run cold as we stand there holding each other. I turn off the shower and get out, wrapping Hadley in a towel when she follows me.

As we get in bed a few minutes later, I finally feel at peace with everything going on in my life.

"You look like you have something on your mind," Hadley says as she trails her fingers up and down my torso.

"What do you think about permanently moving in with me? I've still been paying your apartment so if you want to go back there, I'm not going to stop you. However, if you want to be here, I want you to be here. So much."

Hadley gives me a smile that makes my heart skip a beat. "I think we're already past the point of asking me to move in with you."

"Is that a yes?"

She kisses my shoulder. "I can't think of anyone else I would rather spend forever with."

As we settle down for the night, I hold her tight in my arms, kissing every inch of her that I can reach. She laughs and cuddles up to me, her eyes closing as she puts her head on my chest.

When I run my fingers along her spine, tracing patterns on her skin, I know she was right when she said that every-thing happens for a reason.

My life has been shit, but all of those horrible things led me to my forever.

EPILOGUE
HADLEY

ONE YEAR LATER

"We can't spend forever in the house," I say as I carry another box of children's books to the door. "I only have the rest of the afternoon to finish setting up my classroom and Kennedy has been watching Giovanna for a while already."

Jovan chuckles as he carries my office chair into the front hall. "We're going to get back with plenty of time. I'm sure Kennedy will be fine with watching Giovanna for a few more hours."

"Watching a baby is a lot," I say, stopping in the hall to look over my shoulder at him. "I don't want to have her and Rio looking after our daughter for too long. You know she hates napping."

"Our daughter is fine and Kennedy knows how to take care of her." Jovan puts down the chair and walks over to me, spinning me around and pushing me up against a wall. "It could be worse. Alessio could be the one watching her."

My mouth drops open. "Giovanna may never recover from that. Thankfully, Alessio has already dealt with his insurgents, but I doubt he wants to deal with a baby."

Alessio is still trying to hunt down Paolo Marino. The last thing he needs is a baby to deal with. He has to focus on keeping control of Atlanta before the man he used to call an older brother destroys it.

I wouldn't want to be in his shoes.

"Good, so stop worrying about her for one night and focus on me."

I grin as he looks down at me, his gaze dropping to my mouth. Heat rushes to my core as he takes my wrists in one hand and holds them above my head. Jovan kisses my neck before nipping at my earlobe.

"What do you think about trying for baby number two, kitten?" he asks, his voice husky as he presses his hips against me.

His cock strains against his shorts, brushing against me as he sucks on the sensitive skin at the base of my neck.

"You're trying to distract me. We have things we're supposed to be doing."

Jovan nips at me. "Shut up and enjoy the orgasms like the good little slut that you are."

All thoughts leave me at the dirty talk. He knows exactly what to say and do to make me desperate for him.

I moan as his mouth captures mine in a searing kiss. Our tongues tangle as we strip away our clothing, tossing it away until we're naked. My pussy pulsates as Jovan slides his hands up and down my body. He grabs my hips and pulls me against him harder, guiding us into the living room.

"Bend over the couch and put your ass in the air," he says, his voice gruff as he spins me around. "I want to see that pussy dripping wet."

I moan and arch my back as I bend over the couch. His fingers slide into me as his thumb presses against my clit.

Jovan rocks his fingers back and forth, driving them deeper into me until my legs are shaking.

My nipples ache from brushing against the couch as he thrusts his fingers. My inner walls clench around him as his hand smacks my ass.

"Come for me, kitten."

His fingers move faster as my orgasm comes hard and fast. My pussy is still clenching as he slides out his fingers and replaces them with his cock.

His groan sends shivers down my spine as he slams into me. His fingers dig hard into my hips as he rocks his hips. His cock throbs as he uses one hand to pull back my head by my hair.

My back arches more as I hold onto the couch, trying to take everything he has to give.

"Fuck, I love the way your pussy milks my cock," he says as he rolls his hips, driving himself deeper into me.

Wetness pools between my legs as another orgasm starts to build. He lets go of my hair and smooths his hand down my body, lighting a fire everywhere he touches. His fingers circle my clit, sending me over the edge of another orgasm.

"Fuck yes, kitten, come all over my cock."

He keeps thrusting, drawing out my orgasm for as long as possible before his cock pulses as he stiffens, burying himself to the hilt as he comes.

Jovan trails a line of kisses down my spine before he pulls out and helps me straighten up. He smiles at me with love shining bright in his eyes.

"Want to take a shower and then we can go back to setting up your classroom?" Jovan grins as he pulls me in for a quick kiss. "Or we could spend the rest of the day in bed and working on the next baby."

I laugh and roll my eyes. "As much as I love you and would be thrilled with spending the entire day in bed, I have work that needs to get done before the new school year starts."

He chuckles and picks me up, tossing me over his shoulder. "Shower and back to the school it is."

It's nearly dinner time by the time we finish setting up the classroom. I decided a few weeks ago that I wanted a safari-themed classroom for my first year of teaching kindergarten. Jovan's been more than helpful in setting up the classroom. He's spent the last couple of days moving around desks in every configuration I could picture.

"It looks amazing in here," I say as I look at the animals on the wall and the tall fake grass that climbs up from the ground. "Do you think that the kids are going to love it?"

"I'm sure that they are." Jovan smiles and kisses my cheek. "I'm so proud of you, Hadley. You're going to be a great teacher."

My cheeks warm as I look up at him. "Thank you for everything that you've done to help me. None of this would have been possible without you."

"I love you, Hadley." He steps in front of me and reaches into his pocket. "And I was starting to think about our future. We've been together a while and we have a beautiful daughter together. I love our little family, but I was thinking that there's something missing."

"What's that?" I ask as he pulls a ring out of his pocket and gets to one knee in front of me.

Even though I knew this would be coming someday,

something about seeing him get on one knee has my emotions running wild. My vision starts to blur as I look down at him.

"I told you that I was going to marry you one day. You make me a better man. Every day, you challenge me to be better and do better. I thought most of my life was over before I met you. You gave me so much to live for. Now I'm eager to live every day, wake up every morning with you by my side. Forever. I love you, Hadley. Will you marry me?"

"Yes."

Tears roll down my cheeks as he slips the ring onto my finger. My hands are shaking as he stands up and hugs me, spinning me around in a tight circle. I laugh and hug him, kissing him as he sets me down on the ground.

"I love you so damn much, Hadley."

"I love you too." I wipe away my tears before kissing him again. "I can't believe we're going to get married. Holy shit. We're going to spend the rest of our lives together."

He laughs and shakes his head. "I'm pretty sure we were already planning on doing that."

As I look up at him, my heart soaring, I realize how far my life has come. I went from the teenager sleeping in a car to the woman working to save children who are like her.

I have a fiancé and a daughter. I have a house and a teaching career. I've gotten everything I've ever wanted. Now, I have the rest of my life with Jovan to look forward to.

Thinking about everything that's changed in the last year makes tears well in my eyes again.

"What are you thinking about right now?" Jovan asks before he kisses my forehead.

I smile up at him, basking in the feeling of being loved by him.

"That life with you by my side is going to be a pretty great adventure."

Printed in Great Britain
by Amazon

45604779R00138